How to Hook
a Hottie

also by Tina Ferraro

Top Ten Uses for an Unworn Prom Dress

How to Hook a Hottie

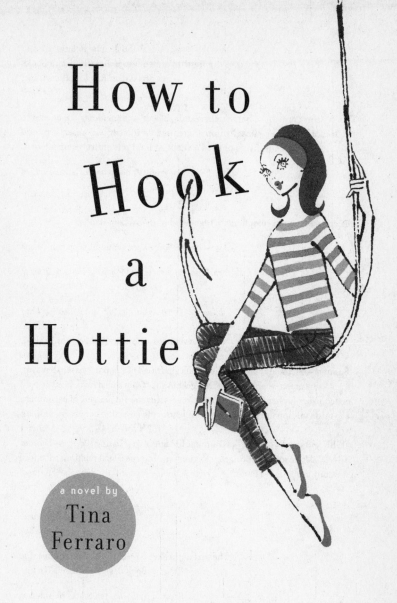

a novel by
Tina Ferraro

Delacorte Press

Published by Delacorte Press
an imprint of Random House Children's Books
a division of Random House, Inc.
New York

Delacorte Press and colophon are registered trademarks of Random House, Inc.

Visit us on the Web! www.randomhouse.com/teens

Educators and librarians, for a variety of teaching tools, visit us at
www.randomhouse.com/teachers

Library of Congress Cataloging-in-Publication Data
Ferraro, Tina.
How to hook a hottie / Tina Ferraro.—1st ed.
p. cm.
Summary: Suddenly and unwillingly the girlfriend of a popular baseball player,
seventeen-year-old Kate DelVecchio goes from social invisibility to paid
matchmaker for her fellow students, progressing toward her goal of becoming a
self-made millionaire by age twenty while proving herself to her absent mother.
ISBN 978-0-385-73438-7 (trade)
ISBN 978-0-385-90444-5 (Gibraltar lib. bdg.) [1. Dating services—Fiction.
2. Moneymaking projects—Fiction. 3. Interpersonal relations—Fiction.
4. Family problems—Fiction. 5. High schools—Fiction. 6. Schools—Fiction.]
I. Title.
PZ7.F365How 2008
[Fic]—dc22
2007012861

The text of this book is set in 12.5-point Filosofia.
Book design by Angela Carlino

Printed in the United States of America

10 9 8 7 6 5 4 3 2 1

First Edition

With special thanks to author Kelly Parra, who got behind this story from day one and believed in it (and in me).

To my incomparable editor, Krista Marino, and agent, Nadia Cornier, for again offering help and expertise.

To the Looney Binners, who are always there with creativity and support.

To the St. James gang, who keep my embers glowing.

To longtime friends Janet Foglia, Donna Herrera, and Magdalena Lear. And to my new friend, author Janie Emaus, who I swear I've known forever.

And finally, to my in-house hotties: Robert, Patrick, and Nick.

For my daughter, Sarah,
who is never too busy to listen,
and who, despite good cause,
is rarely embarrassed by me

How to Hook a Hottie

One

"So, you and the baseball player," prodded the twelve-year-old in the backseat of my car. "Is it *true*?"

My body tensed. Lexie Hoppenfeffer's mother might be paying me to drive her kid to the ice-skating rink and back each weekday afternoon, but that hourly wage did not cover divulging details of my personal life. Especially not answers to questions I couldn't even understand how she knew to ask. And couldn't really understand myself.

"None of your business," I said, glaring in the rearview mirror.

"It *is* true." She giggled. "Don't you even want to know how I heard?"

Yeah. "No."

"Sally's older sister is a sophomore at Franklin Pierce. She said everybody is talking about you and Brandon Callister." She let out this exaggerated sigh and pressed the back of her hand against her forehead. Then she laughed. "I told her *no way*. That the Kate DelVecchio *I* knew wasn't even all that nice, let alone hot enough for a guy like him."

Rolling up to a yield sign, I braked hard. Lexie jerked forward against her seat belt. "Be sure to tell her," I said, catching a glimpse of her baby blues again, "that I'm a terrible driver, too."

She gave me a yeah-yeah squint.

I grinned. Probably for the first time since the baseball hotshot had asked me to the athletic banquet.

The crazy thing had gone down during chem lab. Brandon had been bored—as usual. Talking at me, messing around. The very reason, I'm sure, the chem teacher—who was also the baseball coach—had made us lab partners. I'm no brainiac, but I make up for my shortage of gray matter with determination. I have a personal agenda for acing every class, and nothing and nobody is going to get in my way. Not even some attention-challenged jock.

The whole fall quarter, I'd managed to effectively ignore Brandon and get our work turned in. Then came our much-needed Christmas break, and now we were in the January premidterm grind. Which was probably why he'd started ratcheting things up. Saying things about my hair being pretty (uh-huh, shoulder-length, medium brown, *real* special), my eyes sparkling (brown—double special), and my mouth being beautiful (yeah, right—it's teeth, lips, tongue—check).

Eventually, he got on my last nerve. He claimed he had to present the football MVP award since he'd won last year's baseball MVP ("Tradition, babe") and I just *had* to go with him.

Oh, puh-lease. Didn't he know I didn't date outside my own species?

But instead of stooping to his level, I blew out a sigh and called his bluff. I said sure, whatever, I'd pull something baggy and beige from my mom's closet and go with him. If he'd just shut up.

Amazingly, he did.

I'd turned back to examine the salt water in the crucible, wondering how he'd squirm his way out of the invite. But to my further astonishment, after class, he'd sauntered through the throng of almost three thousand people to the student store and bought the banquet tickets, going as far as telling the clerk—one-man PA system Carlton Camp—that I was his date.

I had shown up at my locker before lunch to see the Who's Who of our Rolling Hills, Washington, high school waiting to check me out, with arched brows and question marks in their eyes. Was it *true* that Brandon and I were now a couple?

3

All that was missing was the Spokane network TV affiliate.

"You're not denying it," Lexie announced now from the backseat. "This is so great. My chauffeur and Brandon Callister."

I bit the inside of my cheek. I'd told her a gazillion times I was not her chauffeur. I was her escort. Or her babysitter. But whatever. I guess it was nice that *somebody* was getting something out of this date.

I was sure that by now Brandon was in total regret mode. His act had blown up in his face, and he was stuck with me. Me—president of the Future Business Leaders of America club. Big whoop to a guy who would forever bask in the glory of having taken our baseball team to its first-ever championship.

Although I failed to see his sex appeal, I was apparently in the minority. Ever since he and Summer Smith had split, the prettiest of the pretty and the most popular of the popular had been cat-scratching to cuddle up to him. I could think of four or five girls off the top of my head who'd trade their Louis Vuitton bags for a date with him.

And *that*'s what I'd say to him tomorrow. (More or less.) Joke's over, ha ha, you won. If you really need a date, ask one of your perfectly accessorized hangers-on.

He'd be relieved. Sure he would. And I'd feel the release of some of this air in my overstuffed lungs. I'd be glad to have my (private) life back, to be back on track for the things I wanted and I'd planned.

The only person who'd be disappointed was Lexie. And somehow that thought made tomorrow's back-out all the sweeter.

Shuffling into the Winter Wonderland locker room minutes later, Lexie realized she'd left her water bottle in the backseat of my car.

"Go get it," she said.

While retrieval was technically part of my job description, no way I was putting up with her attitude. I rolled my eyes so high I could practically see my hairline, and told her to chill.

"*Hurry*. I'm thirsty, Kate."

"Somehow I know you'll live until I get back."

Frowning, I reminded myself—for the hundredth time—that I didn't work for little Lexie. I was contracted by her overprotective and overextended bigtime-romance-author mother, who happened to have an overabundance of cash with which to make sure her precious sweetums was properly coddled.

Cash I was more than happy to take. This job wasn't about pride. It was about empowerment.

The capital I pocketed was going to help make all my dreams come true. Help me burst from my graduation robe in June to reveal a sleek business suit. And put me on course to fulfill my carefully prepared plans. My destiny.

To become a self-made millionaire by twenty.

And just like I wasn't letting Brandon derail my

chem grade, I wasn't letting some bratty twelve-year-old stand in my way, either. Even if it meant biting my tongue until it almost bled.

Crossing the parking lot in the fading daylight, my breath making wispy clouds in the cold air, I trudged back toward my Honda, past SUVs and mom-vans. Bright, attractive, with the ability to be idle or be a powerhouse, my car was a symbol of what I planned to be. If I could just stay on course for another six months, getting the grades and socking away the bucks.

"Hey, you!" a deep voice from down the row startled me back to reality. "Whatcha doing?"

I didn't need to look up, but I did anyway. Jason Dalrymple had had the same husky voice since kindergarten, back when he used to dare me to time-out-worthy pursuits like eating jarred paste and aiming for kids dumb enough to stand at the bottom of the playground slide.

His voice was deeper now. His eyebrows were darker. He was several feet taller. Even his name had evolved. He'd gone from being Jason when we were little to J-Dal in middle school. And now, with so many Jasons roaming the high school halls (and no need for J-Dals), he went simply by Dal.

These days he had far better things to do with his energy than try to get me in trouble. In fact, he was the one who'd hooked me up with Mrs. Hoppenfeffer. He worked at Winter Wonderland, helping fund his hockey "habit" and saving for college, as well as splurging on the occasional weekend trip to see his University of Washington girlfriend.

He and Marissa Penny had been together since last year, when she'd been a senior at Franklin Pierce. The whole thing had started as a dare—Dal had wanted to go to the homecoming dance, and I'd called him a coward for asking me and not trying to get a "real" date. Hours later, he'd strutted up and told me he was going with Marissa. I'd patted his shoulder and told him "Good going," and to this day acted happy for him that the date had blossomed into such a beautiful relationship. Still, sometimes I wished I'd kept my mouth shut. Not because I wanted *my* hands on him, but because I liked being the only girl in his life.

My best-friend jealousy had eased up when Marissa went off to college, except on mornings after he'd been away to see her. When he'd go on and on about how much fun they'd had, how great campus life was. Yada yada yada.

I was *not* into going to college and I was *not* into spending weekends without my best friend, so those mornings, I pretty much had to zip my lip until he changed the subject.

Grabbing Lexie's water bottle from my backseat, I held it up. "The Rink Rat sent me back to the car to get this."

He knocked some dark strands out of his eyes. His hair was usually a mess of bed-head curls and angles, but today it actually looked combed. Imagine that.

"Yeah, what a bummer if she got parched." A smile tugged at his mouth. "Although I'd think that someone who was going to a sports banquet with Brandon Callister would be above such a menial task."

I felt my mouth drop open. Give me a break. Not him, too!

He knew Brandon and I were lab partners. He couldn't have been as electrically shocked as the people who didn't know me or how I could have risen to such awe-inspiring, Brandon-worthy heights.

"Oh, please, Dal," I said, putting just enough disgust into my tone to get my point across.

"It's bull, then?"

I stared into his eyes, which he called hazel but which were known to change with the light and his moods. Right now they were sort of pine green. But I couldn't read the emotion behind them.

"Nope, totally true. He asked me during lab. I thought he was just messing around, and I told him sure, and that I'd wear something from my mother's closet." I grinned, but Dal didn't.

"So that's your out, then. It was just a joke."

My "out"? Okay, getting out was what I'd been thinking. But why had Dal jumped to that conclusion? Brandon was the prize most girls wanted. Why wouldn't I?

"You're all wrong for each other," he said, as if tapping into my thoughts.

True. Starting with the fact that Brandon was all

about basking in his today, while I was all about the future. But that didn't mean I cared to have my closest friend point out how mismatched we were. As if to say Brandon was all that—and I was, well, all not?

I turned to lock my car door and fell into step beside him. The chilly air crept through the openings of my black peacoat, and I struggled to conceal a shiver.

Finally, Dal's voice cut through the silence. "What would you two even talk about? His stats? How much beer he drank at some idiot's party? Come *on*. Is this the right guy for Complikate?"

"Ha ha, very funny," I said, and bumped his shoulder with mine. Using my freshman nickname (bestowed on me by a teacher who'd said I asked too many questions) was hitting below the belt. Even though he had a point.

We'd talk about my hair, I thought. My eyes, my mouth. Ha! But no need to go there. So I shrugged, as if admitting he was right. Which he was, of course. And Dal would be among the first to know that I planned to put an end to the date.

I just wouldn't tell him right now.

As payback for automatically assuming a hot-stuff baseball player and I were mismatched, I wanted him to squirm a little.

Reaching the building, Dal grabbed the front door handle and tugged it open, ushering me in. I glided under his extended arm, moving within inches of his collared Winter Wonderland shirt, and through the door. Then I moved inside without a word or a glance back.

Lexie was doing warm-up laps around the ice when I spotted her, so I set her water bottle down on the team's bench.

I climbed up to my home away from home, the top bleacher on the south side of the building. That was where you could find me pretty much five afternoons a week, along with my cell phone, schoolbooks, reading materials, and laptop. My portable office, as I liked to say.

I'd barely booted up my computer when footsteps thundered up the risers. Another of the rink's employees who also went to Franklin Pierce, Chelsea Mead, was making her way toward me. She had a great smile and a great figure, when she bothered to showcase it, but she always wore at least a couple of bulky T-shirts under her uniform polo shirt, and now her makeup-free cheeks were blotchy from running.

"Checking out dresses for the banquet?" she asked by way of hello.

God! Didn't *anything else* happen in the world today?

"Actually, I was about to check out the S and P Five Hundred and the Dow Jones."

She paused, then did a yeah-right laugh.

Funny—people always thought that was a joke.

Resting a sneaker on the bleacher bench below me, she leaned closer. "Kate, can I talk to you?"

"Sure. Unless it's about Brandon."

"Oh, uh," she stammered. "Not really. Well, kinda." She inhaled. "Okay, here goes. I want a date to the football banquet, too. With a *particular* player. And I want to know how you pulled it off. You know, what you did to get Brandon to ask you."

What I did? Like sprinkled fairy dust? Or maybe . . . snuck into his house, stole his Seattle Mariners autographed baseball, and refused to give it back unless he took me to an über-boring, rubber-chicken-on-a-plate banquet? Puh-lease! The general public's disbelief was definitely getting to me.

"My brother's on JV," she went on, "so my parents are making me go. And it would just be sooo much better if I was sitting with *this guy* instead of them."

"So tell him," I said, in no way missing the irony that I had accepted a date to the very same banquet because it was easier than saying no.

"No way," she said. "I couldn't. Besides, players ask girls to this thing. Not the other way around." She seemed to swallow hard. "I need your help. How do I let him know I want to go—if he'd only ask, I'd totally say yes. I mean, what did you say to convince Brandon to ask you?"

"Convince?"

"Oh," she said, and waved a dismissive hand. "That's not really what I meant. You know."

Yeah, I knew. And I *so* wanted to tell her where to stuff it. But our paths crossed all the time here at

Winter Wonderland and occasionally at school, and business lecturers advised keeping personal feelings on the back burner whenever possible. "I'm sorry. But I couldn't—"

"I'll pay you," she said, tugging on the hem of her collective shirt. "Whatever it costs."

My denial died on my tongue.

"Fifty up front," she went on. "Fifty more if he asks me."

Fifty big ones just for saying yes? Huh. I had to waste two afternoons with Lexie to make that much. And if I could pull it off . . .

Not bad, I thought, not bad at all.

The thing was—to be fair—what did I know about getting a guy to ask a girl out? I hadn't done a thing to snag Brandon, unless you counted our lab assignments. And while I'd had a boyfriend for a while in tenth grade, this guy had pursued me.

Still, odds were I knew more than Chelsea, or she wouldn't be asking. Maybe what she really needed most was a shot in the arm to boost her confidence. And she'd get just that from believing I was there for her.

Fifty. Maybe a hundred.

"That's a lot of money, Chelsea."

"He's worth every penny."

And I would be happy to *take* every penny. Part of my rise-to-the-top strategy was to access any and all business prospects that came my way, looking for the real moneymakers, or what the movers and shakers called "Ideal Opportunities." So far, my opportunities had been restricted to driving a spoiled kid around, but a person had to keep her options open.

"Sit down," I said, and patted the spot beside me on the bench. "Let's talk more about this." I closed my laptop and sat up straight, giving her my full attention.

"Oh, I can't right now. I've got to get back to work. But how about tonight on the phone? Like about seven o'clock?"

I nodded, retrieved one of my custom-made business cards from my backpack ("Kate DelVecchio, Entrepreneur"), and handed it to her. Then I scribbled her number in a notebook.

"So we're on?" she asked, and let free that hundred-watt smile that I knew would be my cash cow.

"We're on."

I flipped my laptop back open and clicked to a search engine. I had about one hour to learn how to attract guys—something that had managed to elude me for all my seventeen years.

Good thing I liked a challenge.

Two

With tips like "Focus on him, not on yourself" and "Keep the conversation a two-way street" floating through my head, I maneuvered my way down the bleacher steps and toward the snack bar after Lexie's practice ended. Dal, Chelsea, and a white-blond junior named Mark Bergstrom were hustling cold drinks and hot dogs to calorie-depleted skaters, and I called out a generic goodbye.

Chelsea caught my eye and mouthed "Seven."

I nodded, then spotted Lexie leaning against the wall of the foyer, her skates dangling from one hand, her practice clothes in a loose ball in the other. I'd told her a dozen times she should get one of those carryalls like the other girls had, but all that had netted me was more of her superior nose wrinkles.

Such a charming kid.

And she *was* still a kid, even though she tried to act like she was ready to pledge a sorority. All I had to do was make a roll of Life Savers appear in my hand and her face lit up.

I half wondered if her rush to grow up had to do with being an only child, or if she'd simply been born on a fast track.

But then, who was I to talk? I spent more hours catching up on back issues of *Business Week* than I did reading teen mags or my yearbook.

Amanda Hoppenfeffer, known to me as Mrs. H., was standing in the circular driveway when we pulled up. A sprawling two-story colonial with more bathrooms than my house had bedrooms lay behind her, a giant Douglas fir stretching its bushy arms up from the backyard. Mrs. H.'s auburn hair was swept back into a casual bun, and her arms were weighed down by plastic grocery sacks.

Seeing her bags reminded me that my sister had called my cell to ask me to pick up a block of cheddar. I loved my Honda, but it had turned me into a delivery service.

"Oh, Kate!" Mrs. H. called.

Lexie barreled out of the backseat without a word to me, which was no problem—I'd heard enough of that kid's voice to last a lifetime. Mrs. H. took some labored steps toward her daughter, then passed her completely in her journey to my passenger window.

Feeling a twinge of sympathy for Lexie, I powered down the window. I *really* wasn't in the mood for one of her sermons on the safest driving routes or how she didn't want Lexie to get overheated, so I hoped this would be fast.

"Kate," she began, an icy blast blowing through the open window. "I heard the oddest thing today."

Omigod. This wasn't about Lexie. This was about me. And Brandon. The gossip mill here in Rolling Hills was freaking ridiculous!

"Apparently this year's qualifying competitions aren't going to be in Seattle after all, but in New York City."

I bit back a laugh. "Really," I said, for once more than happy to talk about her snotty daughter. "Why's that?"

"You got me. But with airfare, hotel, costumes, and all the other fees, it's going to run *thousands* of dollars instead of hundreds."

I just nodded. I figured she wanted sympathy, but sorry, none available. My idea of a big splurge was a Big Mac. Hers was to see Big Ben.

"Did you hear anything about it at the rink today? Other mothers complaining?"

I tapped my fingers on the steering wheel, pretending to be thinking back. Did she honestly think I hung with the mothers? I was tempted to tell her how I'd truthfully earned most of today's pay—trying to figure out how to dump one of the school's hottest seniors and how to hook the guy of the snack bar girl's dreams. Except I liked her money too much.

"Sorry, Mrs. H. I didn't hear a thing. But Lexie might know something," I said, encouraging the lady to do what she should have been doing anyway: *talk to her kid*.

Mrs. H. nodded her dismissal and I took my cue. I didn't need to be reminded that I was officially off the clock.

The supermarket was out of my way, but it wasn't like I had a choice. With my mother working on her PhD in Germany, each remaining member of the family had specific jobs: Dad made the money and paid the bills, my sister Suzannah did the cooking, and I handled the errands.

I figured I was getting off pretty easy, so if it meant shifting and sighing in cashier lines now and then—well, no real complaints. Besides, the errands were the reason I'd gotten my Honda last February. My mother had ordered it online and made sure it arrived on the morning of my seventeenth birthday.

My friends had oohed and aahed—at least, the ones with good taste had—but anyone who knew what was going on inside the walls of our house knew the real truth behind the car. It had been a "hush" gift, a way for Pamela DelVecchio to wipe her long-distance-responsibility slate clean while she blazed a new and more exciting trail.

I had considered refusing the car and telling my mother where to shove it. But the car meant freedom, including the end to embarrassing school drop-offs in our dad's hideous plumbing truck. On top of that, Dal mentioned a certain Mrs. Hoppenfeffer waving cash around the rink to attract a suitable driver for her kid. Plus, the Honda was *adorable*. I customized it with flowered seat covers and things dangling from the rearview mirror.

And so what do you know? Mom and I actually had a meeting of the minds on the car. But like mother, like daughter?

No. *Nein*. No way, Jose.

In fact, a driving force behind my Millionaire Before Twenty plan was to prevent me from ever, even accidentally, turning into a put-yourself-first wife and mother like her. I'd do my own thing *before* I started a family—or even *thought* of starting one.

(Bitter much? Who—me?)

The second I walked into the kitchen I was attacked for my cheese.

"The cheddar!" Suzannah exclaimed when I dropped the plastic bag on the kitchen table. "Cheeseburgers just aren't cheeseburgers without cheese."

"Yeah, they're called hamburgers." I climbed onto a counter stool and blew some loose strands of hair away from my face. Traffic had been slow on Division Boulevard, but I'd managed to make it home before the cheese got all soft and gooey from the front seat heater.

"I figured we'd have your favorite tonight. Because you'd either be celebrating or needing comfort food."

I searched her face. Suz had the same straight, dark hair I did, but fuller lips and higher cheekbones. Now that she wore contacts instead of her clunky glasses, she was really pretty. But I'd never tell *her* that. She was two years younger than me and I had to keep her humble. "I take it you heard."

"People started mentioning it to me at lunch, and by the time I got to water polo practice, I was practically a celebrity by association."

"Yeah. I'm half expecting a story on CNN tonight." I rested my chin on my folded arms. "So what are people thinking? Is it bad?"

"Not so bad, really. Either you've grown on Brandon during chem lab, which means you're not as invisible and boring as people originally thought . . ."

That wasn't bad?

"Or you threatened not to do his lab work anymore unless he took you. So he had no choice."

My head jerked up. "And what—getting his coach to give him a new lab partner wasn't an option? Don't these people *think*?" I frowned. "Anyway, it's more like I told him I'd go with him *so* I could get his work done."

Suzannah looked confused—which was one of the few things today that made sense—so I explained.

"So you meant it as a joke," she concluded, "but you're going anyway, right?"

"I'll get out of it somehow. Tomorrow."

"*Why?*"

"He's annoying."

"He's hot!" she said, and followed with a what-*is*-your-problem scoff.

"He's immature."

"So jump his bones so he can't talk."

I rolled my eyes.

"I don't get you," Suzannah said, scrunching her face. "This is like winning the lottery. I mean, *Brandon Callister*. Totally popular, buff, and did I mention hot?"

I paused, thinking about Brandon's unremarkable face and the ears that were pressed so tight against his head they got lost in his hair. I wondered if she'd think he was so hot without all the baseball buzz.

"And you're going to pass this date up, Kate. To do what? Analyze the bond market or something just as stupid?"

Actually, I'd been thinking about a movie with Dal and some friends, but her idea was good, too. So I nodded.

She made a pistol out of her thumb and forefinger and aimed it at my head. "You, Katharine DelVecchio, are too stupid to live." She pulled the imaginary trigger. "Bang, bang. No cheeseburger."

"Then you," I said, and lunged for the supermarket bag, "don't get the cheese."

That was where Dad found us, moments later. On the kitchen floor, laughing with a block of cheddar cheese between us. Our mother would have gone all rigid and disapproving, probably said things about ruining our clothes and our complexions—not to mention the cheese. But Dad just looked sort of baffled, probably not sure if this was some female bonding ritual or if we had temporarily changed into six-year-old boys. (For the record, the answer was both.)

"When's dinner, Suzannah?" he asked, propping his metal lunchbox on the counter as if this was how he normally found us. His lunchbox was scratched and dented from years of being banged around inside his truck, but Dad wouldn't dream of getting a new one any more than he'd dream of buying his lunch.

Not that money was the issue. Dad's business was booming, and more than once, I'd heard our mother suggest he sell it and invest the profits in real estate or other ventures. But that wasn't Dad. He was happiest when snaking drains, laying pipes, and doing all that messy, hands-on stuff. He was oceans away from our mother. Figuratively, as well as literally.

I let Suz crawl out from under my hold.

"Twenty minutes, Dad," she managed to reply, her face flushed. "I just need to fry the burgers."

"Okay," he said. "I'm taking a shower."

I glanced at the wall clock. I needed to get my

English homework started before dinner, considering I had that phone call later.

I stood and shook a finger at my sister. "*This* is not over."

"Not in a million years."

A smile tugged at her mouth and she went back to forming hamburger patties, probably hoping this was one of the times she could count on Big Sister's hand-me-downs, but not fully grasping that Brandon wasn't mine to pass off and never would be.

Being popular and running with the "cool kids" just didn't get my motor running. Which either made me wise beyond my years or just plain weird.

Three

Belly-down on my bed after dinner, one hand poised above my laptop keyboard, the other on my cell phone, I listened to the ringing on the other end.

I hadn't bothered to ask Chelsea who her so-called hottie was, but circumstances being what they were, that wasn't so odd. You see, many, many housing developments ago—way before the rush of people discovered the crisp, clean air and wide-open spaces in eastern Washington—Franklin Pierce High School had been built to hold about a thousand students.

The community might have grown, but Franklin

Pierce hadn't. Now we were two and three to a locker, up to forty in a class. (Any wonder a petition had gone around last year to change our school mascot from Spartans to Sardines?) As if making a name for yourself wasn't hard enough at *any* high school, you pretty much had to be a beauty queen, a sports legend, or a delinquent awaiting trial to get noticed around here.

Which explained a lot about my current situation:

How I could be a Rolling Hills native, have near-perfect school attendance and a very decent 3.6 GPA, be prez of a recognized club, and still wander the hallways anonymously.

How a goof-off like Brandon had attained a godlike status with his golden pitching arm.

And why I hadn't bothered to ask Chelsea to reveal her secret crush. I mean, what were the odds I'd even heard of the guy?

After what felt like an eternity, Chelsea answered, and I quickly shifted to my professional tone—the one I practiced in the car when pretending to be interviewing with corporate CEOs.

I started by asking her how well she knew the guy. "Are we talking a total stranger here? Or someone you speak to?"

"I know him. Really well. He works at the rink."

I started to say, "Good." But everything inside me suddenly tensed and my words tumbled out. "It wouldn't happen to be Dal, right?"

"No."

"Because Dal has a girlfriend."

"I told you . . ."

"And he's a dedicated guy, wouldn't cheat or anything."

". . . that he's a football player," she continued.

"Yeah, right." I inhaled, trying to hear her. But just one more thing, almost because I needed to hear it myself. "Because Dal's a really good friend of mine, and it would be unethical, as well as just plain dishonest of me, to plot something behind his and Marissa's back."

"Mark," she finally blurted out.

Then she let out this dreamy sigh that felt embarrassingly personal, so I basically ignored it and stayed with the program.

Mark was good. Very good. Not only did she know him, but I did, too. He was the tall blond I'd seen working beside her in the snack bar. I could watch his reactions to her. Get a feel for whether I could bring this job to its rightful conclusion.

Wait—better yet, what if I brought Dal in on it? As my inside man, he could work on Mark while I worked on Chelsea. Sure, I'd have to slip Dal some bucks, but every business had its outlay expenses. And I knew he needed money for college.

Dal . . . yeah. Good.

When my mind connected with Chelsea's voice again, she was still all about Mark. How cute he was, how he didn't have a girlfriend, how she just knew they'd be perfect together, et cetera, et cetera. I just hoped she didn't ramble this much around him.

"So, what do you think?" she finally paused to ask. "Can you make it work for us?"

I sat up and balanced my laptop on my crossed legs. "I'm going to have to do more research and crunch the numbers," I said, because it sounded good. "See if you and Mark fit into my . . . my . . . you know, Six-Point Plan. My, uh, hottie-hooking *hexagon*."

"Oh, Kate, I knew it! You *do* have some secret formula or something. Omigod, this is so great. You're really going to make this happen for me."

I managed a smile, praying I'd never have to explain myself. A hottie-hooking hexagon? I could hear the buzzer blaring on my BS meter. Fortunately—and more importantly—Chelsea didn't seem to. She promised to bring me fifty big ones the next day and then wondered aloud if she'd be able to sleep.

I wondered the same about myself. I mean, she only had anticipation to deal with. I was the one flying without a net.

Suzannah and I were crossing the senior parking lot the next morning when the first bell sounded. Good thing I pretty much carried my entire life in my backpack, because there was no time for my locker.

I rushed through the side door and tugged off my knit cap. Following a full hair flick and some pats to combat the static, I headed off in the direction of my first classroom, going into my usual corridor routine—shove, "Excuse me," push, "Sorry."

But something strange happened. Instead of moving in fits and starts, the crowd parted away from me—or *for* me—letting me pass. People stopped, turned. And stared.

And then there were the voices—some whisper quiet, some loud and obnoxious.

"That's *her*."

"Brandon's new girlfriend . . ."

"Kate DelVecchio."

It was like one of those dreams where people are gawking at you and it takes you a while to realize you're naked.

"DelVecchio's no dog," a girl said as I rounded a corner. "But she's no Summer Smith, either."

That voice was instantly recognizable. It had blended with mine spring after spring in elementary school when we'd stood outside supermarkets in our Brownie uniforms, hawking Thin Mints and Do-Si-Dos.

I was tempted to look tough-as-nails Dakota Watson dead in the eye and tell her thanks—and that I didn't think she howled at the moon, either. But what was the point? My banquet date was going to be history by lunch, and this embarrassing mess would be nothing but a blip on the radar of my senior year. Plus, she and I still needed to get along in our Future Business Leaders of America club.

Feeling the stares of Dakota and her friends drilling into the back of my peacoat, I continued to class, telling myself not to sweat it. Soon I'd be the only one who even remembered this morning had happened.

To say I was glad to see Dal out on the quad during morning break would be an understatement. I was in dire need of someone who knew me, liked me, and wasn't out to judge me.

And besides, I had that proposal for him.

"Did you break your date from hell yet?" he asked as soon as he saw me.

Okay—I admit I would have preferred a simple "Hi, Kate." And I *still* wasn't thrilled with how he'd somehow gotten all critical of my so-called love life. But the last thing I wanted was more conflict, so I rubbed my chilly palms together and met his gaze. "Not yet."

"What are you waiting for?"

"Next period. When we have chem."

"Oh . . . yeah." He let out a little laugh, then a smile so wide that it touched his eyes.

A couple of his hockey buddies stopped by with a big bag of Flaming Hot Cheetos. Which was great—I mean, the more Cheetos the better—until one of them asked about my Big Date. I shot Dal a look, curious to see how he'd respond, and crammed my mouth with artificial cheese.

"Just a misunderstanding," he said, and shrugged. "Brandon and Kate are chem partners. That's all."

I wasn't letting Dal off the hook *that* easily, so when all eyes fell on me, I gave him a little grin and a shrug. Leaving the door open just a little. I was starting to see that the attention Brandon had given me *did* have its uses. . . .

The guys switched to talking hockey—*boring*—so I tuned them out and glanced around the quad. Carlton Camp from the student store was sitting alone on a stoop, staring at a nearby group of girls. They seemed oblivious to him, and I sort of felt sorry for him, until one of the girls caught *me* staring, and then I just felt stupid for myself.

An icy gust of wind suddenly whipped across the quad, doing an Einstein thing to my unhatted hair. Batting it down, I watched a couple of the guys hunch their shoulders against the cold.

The bell rang, and we all said our goodbyes. Dal walked me toward the science wing. I waited until I was sure we couldn't be overheard, then told him about yesterday—how Chelsea had hired me, and how I wanted his help.

Astonishment creased his brow. "You want me to ask Mark if he likes her?"

"Well, I'm hoping you'll be a little smooth about it."

"What's in this for me?"

"Ten bucks."

He turned and studied my face. Holding his gaze, I realized I was fiddling with my hair, which I'm sure meant something deep to body-language professionals but which merely told me I was probably coming off as anxious as I felt. And had probably left Cheeto dust in my bangs.

"Okay," I amended. "Twenty."

He just stared at me—he had me over a barrel and he knew it.

"And," I said, dredging the words up from deep within me, "another ten if I need to use your services to close the deal."

"Another twenty."

"Twenty! Hey, I'm spearheading this. You're just a contractor. And besides, I'm supposed to be saving for my future."

"And I'm not?"

Man, I hated it when he was right. And when my face acknowledged it without my permission. I had no choice but to cave. "Fine."

He studied me. "You backed down too easily, Kate. It's not like you to throw around money."

"What can I say? It looks like an Ideal Opportunity."

He grinned. I knew he wasn't laughing *at* me exactly, more like with me. He'd heard me use that phrase once or twice or a hundred times in the past year. Usually as in *looking for* the Ideal Opportunity.

"Well, then," he said, and seemed to swallow his grin, "if this is an Ideal Opportunity, how can I refuse? But one question: what happens if you end up short at graduation?"

"I figure you'll give it back to me." He didn't laugh, so I did. "No, look, if I'm going to do this, I'm going to do it *right*. And for that, I need your help," I said, and sort of held my breath.

"Okay, but I'm keeping whatever you pay me."

"Only fair," I said, feeling a smile creep to my lips. I'd just passed a test in Business 101. I'd assessed the problems, acknowledged my limitations, found a supplier, and successfully negotiated the contract. "There's enough money out there for both of us."

He stopped at the fork in the path. "Okay, then, I guess I've got a job to do. And you do, too," he said, and nodded toward the science wing. "Go break his heart, baby doll."

I gave him the eye roll he deserved, then walked away, dollar signs still filling my head.

I had more than just the usual hunger for cold, hard cash. At the beginning of the school year, I had talked my parents into signing an unusual agreement: if I raised Five Thousand Big Ones by my graduation and showed them a senior report card with nothing but As, they would—despite what they admitted were the strongest reservations—hand over the balance of my college savings account. Which at last peek was over ten grand.

I knew they'd only scribbled their names to shut me up. They figured I'd fall short financially, and the good grades would help get me into a good college. But more likely, they would learn that they'd underestimated me. Because I didn't do anything halfway, and I didn't take on anything I didn't think I could win.

I would get that money and use it as start-up capital on whatever venture struck me at the time. I'd enter the real world and blaze my own trail, get a jump start on others who'd be wasting four years in college.

Not that I had anything against college. There were obviously worlds of knowledge to be acquired there, connections to be made, good opportunities to take advantage of. But college wasn't the only way.

Look at my dad. With nothing more than a high school diploma, he'd parlayed his plumbing skills into a company so successful that he actually turned work down. And I was my dad's daughter, right?

Besides, I was off to a good start at meeting my end of the deal. My grades were high, and I had about $2,400 in a shoe box under my bed. Paychecks from the Hoppenfeffers would get me to $4,000 by June. I could factor in interest after I brought myself to deposit the cash in a savings account, but right now I was having too much fun looking at it, counting it, playing with it.

The last grand would have to come from somewhere—but I told myself not to worry. I'd earn it. Somehow. I had to. I *could* and I *would* be a player. ASAP.

A hand reached out and grabbed me outside my chem class. I turned to see Chelsea, a look of relief on her face. "Here," she said, and pushed a fistful of bills into the pocket of my coat.

"I thought we'd talk more about this later," I said, but involuntarily, my hand slipped into my pocket and closed around the cash.

"Just make it work, Kate. Seriously."

And she was off into the crowd before I could say another word, leaving me with nothing but fifty bucks and a lingering reluctance to go face my *other* problem.

When I walked into the chem lab, Brandon was already at our table, straddling the back of his chair. For a split second, he held my eye, then he shifted his gaze away.

I was not about to play the I-don't-see-you-either game. We were allegedly friends—or, if you believed the gossip, more than friends—so we had to at least acknowledge each other. "Hey, Brandon."

He glanced up at me. "Oh, hi."

"Did you get the homework done?"

He shrugged. "Two words: 'Xbox.' "

I shook my head and sank down into my seat, pretty sure that "Xbox" was one word.

After a pause long enough for him to have hit a homer and run all the bases, he nudged me. "Uh, Kate?" I looked over. His forehead was wrinkled, his eyes sort of squinty. "About the banquet. We have to talk."

I felt a laugh bubble up inside me, but I wasn't sure

33

if it was from self-congrats (I mean, had I called this one right or what?) or utter embarrassment. Even though he didn't do a thing for me, I didn't want him breaking things off. If the date had made news, the dump would make headlines.

As Coach took attendance, Brandon screeched his chair toward mine until he was so close I could feel his body heat, could breathe in his musky scent. Which wasn't altogether unpleasant. Though it didn't start my engine roaring, either.

"Don't hate me," he said in a half whisper, confirming my suspicions.

I shook my head. I'd have to love him or at least like him before I could hate him, right?

"I told my mom about the banquet last night, and she reminded me that I won't even be here. I'm leaving on Sunday."

Uh-huh. How convenient.

"I'm going to some baseball showcases. You know, where college coaches come to check out high school players."

No, I didn't know. Nor did I necessarily believe him.

"How long will you be gone?" I asked, just because I wanted him to squirm.

"Two weeks. I have to bring homework and stuff." He shrugged. "I mean, I knew I was going, but I forgot how soon. I'm sorry."

I shrugged. "Turns out I had a conflict, too. So I wasn't going to be able to go."

"Oh." He glanced at a poster—as if he cared about electrons—then back at me. "I was going to give you the tickets so you could take a friend or something. But . . ."

His voice trailed off, which was fine with me. All I wanted was this conversation *over*.

That, and another lab partner.

And if the rumor mill transformed this breakup into some humiliating story, I'd probably want another life, too.

But logic told me he was probably telling the truth. I mean, the guy still practically used his fingers to count, so it stood to reason that calendars were over his head.

Then there was the fact that it was beyond stupid to make up a story like that. He'd either be at school these next couple of weeks or he wouldn't.

"Kate," he said, interrupting the hurricane in my brain. "I know this is last minute, but if you're not busy, I thought we could go out tonight instead. Get a pizza. See a movie. Something."

I was too dumbstruck to keep up pretenses. "What? You want to go out . . . for *real*?"

Brandon laughed, way too loud for class. Especially since nothing amusing was happening—or had ever happened—in that particular classroom.

"No, for fake."

I studied his face, my thoughts drifting back. "Was this your mother's idea?"

He shrugged, telling me what I needed to know.

I sat back and bit my lip in consideration. Did I particularly want a date with him?

Uh—no.

But did I want to be the butt of jokes for the rest of my senior year? The geek girl Brandon Callister briefly toyed with before putting her back in her place?

Uh—not even a little bit.

He was probably harmless, anyway. And we were only talking pizza, maybe a movie. One date for the sake of my rep wouldn't kill me, right?

Four

Dal was sweeping the foyer when Lexie and I cruised into the rink later. He wore his navy blue polo shirt and a no-nonsense expression.

"So, Kate," he said, again not bothering with preliminaries. "Did you get the job done?"

"Yes and no," Lexie spoke up.

His gaze fled from mine to hers and back to mine again.

"The banquet date is off," I said. "Brandon has to go to some college baseball tryouts."

He nodded. "I heard about that. I just didn't know it was so soon."

"Apparently, neither did he." I tried to sound like I didn't care, although with all the random people who seemed to know about his road trip, I no longer suspected Brandon had tried to pull a fast one on me.

"Instead," Lexie proudly continued, "she's going out with him *tonight*. They're—"

"Wait," I said, interrupting her before Dal could jump to conclusions. "I figured pizza is the best way to fend off unflattering rumors."

"Besides," Lexie added, standing between us, hanging on my every word. "Brandon is *hot*."

Dal frowned at her. "What do you know? You're like . . . ten."

"I'm twelve," she said, and gave her blond hair a proper toss. "And I *know* hot. Apolo Anton Ohno, Orlando Bloom." She slanted a look at me. "Don't you think Brandon's hot, Kate?"

I shooed Lexie toward the locker room before she and Dal tangled it up good. "You'll be late," I said, trying to ignore her.

"You just don't want to answer me," she charged. "You want me out of here before the good stuff starts. Just like my parents."

"What I want is for you not to have to do penalty laps for being late. Your mother would find out and dock my pay."

She sniffed but headed toward the doorway. I

watched until she cleared it, then I turned back to Dal, whose dark eyes were back to a more human shade of green.

"She asked a good question, Kate. Maybe you *do* think Brandon's hot."

I'd had about enough of this! "Yeah, hot like the desert in the summer. Sweltering, bone-dry, just-get-me-out-of-here hot."

"Oh," he said, his voice taking on a teasing tone. "The kind where you end up practically naked, rubbing lotion on your body?"

I groaned and gave him a bump to knock the smile from his face. "Look, the only thing I'm trying to do is prevent 'Kate DelVecchio Got Dissed' from being the header in hundreds of this weekend's e-mails, okay?"

Suddenly Mr. Serious, Dal narrowed his eyes. "What if you end up having a good time? You could lose sight of everything you've been working for."

A parental tone was never a good one to take with me. "I don't know where this is even coming from, but you know how I feel about him." I frowned. "Besides, I don't see *your* relationship holding you back."

"Marissa and I are different."

Not that I wanted to know anything private about her, but only a coward would back off. "Yeah? How's that?"

His jaw twitched, his expression sharpened, then he shook his head. "We just are."

Oh, *that* helped.

I was tempted to ask if he thought she was hot, but he'd been going out with her for about a year and a half, so I figured that was a given.

"Look," I said, and then *didn't* look at him. "Maybe it's best if we just drop this." After an awkward beat, I pushed on and changed the subject. "I don't suppose you got the chance to talk to Mark?"

"As a matter of fact, I did."

He leaned against his broom handle, making his biceps go all big. Dal had a great body, and I was sure he knew it. But it didn't feel right to check him out—ever. And especially not on top of the talk about Marissa. So I quickly averted my gaze back to his.

"He's going to the banquet," he went on, "and doesn't have a date."

"All right! Now, *that's* what I wanted to hear." I put up my hand and he slapped it. "The big questions are, does he *want* a date, and what does he think of Chelsea?"

"I didn't ask."

"Why not?"

"Well, we can't rush things. We want him to be *into* her, right? Not just looking for a one-nighter."

"Uh, yeah," I said, although honestly, I hadn't thought past arranging the hookup and taking the payment. "Sure."

"So we need to go slow."

I had to give him credit. He'd always aced me out on tests, even back in elementary school. But lately I'd become impressed with his ability to read between the lines, too.

"But not too slow, Dal."

"Yeah, I'll try to work it in today. Maybe drop a few lines about how cute she is, and how she doesn't have a boyfriend."

"He's going to think *you* like her."

"No way. He knows about Marissa."

Marissa again. That girl was like one-size-too-small panties. No matter how hard I tried to ignore her or pretend to be okay with her, she kept reappearing to bite me in the butt.

"Fine—do it your way," I said, and reached into my pocket to dig up his share of the pay. "But ASAP, okay? Clock's ticking." I slipped him his money and finally broke, giving him a little smile.

"Pleasure doing business with you," he said, palming the cash. "Boss."

I opened my mouth to tell him not to call me that, but for some reason, whatever I was going to say just flew out of my head.

As I cruised back through the rink, disembodied voices bounced off the domed ceiling and the walls of Winter Wonderland, tangling with the sounds of scraping blades. Over the past months, I'd grown comfortable with these background noises, come to count on them much the way my dad counted on the lull of the TV.

But the voices were higher and sweeter than usual. I noticed that free skate was ending and little kids and their moms were whooshing and whirly-birding off the ice. Shaking off a memory of my mother and me in some preschool skating class—back when I was young and cute and worthy of her time—I climbed the bleachers.

I was going through my e-mails, deleting junk and a message from my mom, when Chelsea clomped up the staircase again. It was time to get down to business. Her cash was still warming my pocket, and I wanted more.

"Have a seat, Chelsea. I've got great news," I said, knowing I needed to inspire her confidence. "It just so happens that Mark is dateless for the banquet."

I watched her hopeful look turn into that huge smile. "Oh, good! How did you find out?"

I hesitated. Telling her Dal had simply asked seemed so . . . ordinary. Must have been all those *How to Succeed in Business* books I'd thumbed through, but I wanted her to think I was offering a service no one else could provide. "Let's not waste time with my methods now. Just know I'm getting the job done."

She nodded. I guess she thought it sounded good. (I know I did.)

"So here's what's next, Chelsea. I want you to try the wristwatch test."

"The . . . ?"

"Listen up. This is what you're paying me for." I hoped. But according to the Web site where I'd found this test, it was almost always accurate. "You start by complimenting his watch," I said, trying to sound all serious, like this had been created in a lab by some relationship scientist. "And ask to see it."

She nodded, leaning in.

"If he unlatches the band and hands it to you—sorry, as they say, he's just not that into you. But if he offers up his watch, his wrist, his arm? It's simply a matter of how fast and how far you want to take it."

Her hands fled to her mouth.

"So," I said, pointing down at the snack bar. "Go back to work and run the test. And report back to me."

"Totally!" she said. She gave me a quick—and not altogether warranted—hug and skipped down the stairs.

I just hoped I could help her *stay* that happy.

Sighing, I went back to the Internet for a look at how my favorite stocks had fared. I was still undecided as to whether I should invest my money in the market, in an existing company, or create something of my own.

I'd seen a CNN segment on a college student who'd started a multimillion dollar corporation by selling office chairs through the Internet, and I couldn't help admiring the simplicity of his plan. I knew zip about office chairs and had no idea how to design a Web site, but every time I thought about how quickly he'd soared to such heights, I felt this kind of bubbly excitement.

I could do it, too. With the right idea and enough capital, and by keeping my options open.

A heavier, less rhythmic set of footsteps pounded

its ascent up the risers, and suddenly Dal was hovering over me. I was fairly certain his proximity to my face was simply meant to keep him from being overheard, but nonetheless I scooted down the bench a little to ensure enough personal space.

"I told Mark I thought Chelsea was hot," he whispered. "And he was like, 'Dude, you already got a girlfriend.'"

I'll admit I liked being right, but it didn't serve me in this particular case. "I hope you straightened him out."

"As well as I could."

He pulled back. His nose wrinkled and his mouth tugged into this little smile. For an instant, he was five-year-old Jason again. But then he took a deep inhale and blew out the breath, which did amazing things to his so-*not*-little-kid chest.

I reeled in my thoughts. "Okay, time to play our next hand. Chelsea's pretty when she tries. We need to get her cleaned up and get them to meet outside of the rink. Where he can see her as someone other than a snack bar girl."

His lips pursed, he nodded. "I'd suggest tonight, but rumor has it you've got plans."

"Ha ha."

"Tomorrow night?"

"My dad's birthday," I said, shaking my head. Ever since our mother left, Suzannah and I had been making a bigger deal out of birthdays and holidays. We'd thrown an Extreme Christmas, with a prime rib, door-to-door caroling, popcorn garlands, and a mountain of gifts. A psychotherapist would probably say we were over-compensating. My goal was to stir up as much hype as possible and then throw it back in Mom's across-the-ocean face. Suzannah's was probably to make *me* feel better.

"But tomorrow's Saturday—I could do breakfast," I added.

"Is Chelsea a morning person?"

"My guess is she'd stay up all night dancing to a snake charmer's flute if she thought it would get Mark's attention."

"Oh, he'd pay attention, all right," he said, and flashed a grin. "Just not in a good way . . ."

I opened the calendar accessory on my laptop. "Bev's Diner, tomorrow. Say nine? I'll get Chelsea there, you get Mark. We'll 'run into each other.' "

"What? How . . . Why do I get the hard work?"

"Well, you're the guy," I said, for lack of a better answer.

"What does that have to do with it?"

"Next time, if our client is male, I'll have to do all the dirty work."

He shot me a look. "Next time. Yeah, right!"

I quickly assessed my options, then gave him a playful smile. "How about I pick up your breakfast tab? Factor it into this project's budget."

"Budget," he repeated.

"Hey, we're talking fifty more bucks if we can close this deal."

He frowned, then nodded. "Okay, but I swear, Kate, if Mark starts thinking I'm after *him,* I'm blowing the lid on this whole operation."

"Fair enough. And in that case," I said, and waggled my eyebrows, "I promise to do *whatever's necessary* to preserve your reputation."

I laughed like a hyena—Dal and me pretending to be romantically involved was funny, right?—until I realized the only sound coming back to me was the rink roar. Dal just stood there staring blankly at me. I knew he was kidding about Mark thinking he was gay—but did he doubt that I'd rise to any occasion to help him?

No. . . . If Dal and I had anything, it was best-friendship trust.

So what, then? Did he think I was "man enough" to partner in business with, but not "woman enough" to be a flirt if the situation demanded it?

I tensed, that possibility hurting worse than the first; then I quickly pulled myself together and looked back at my computer screen. I was so superbusy I almost missed his mumbled "See ya."

Yeah, fine, whatever.

On my way to snag Lexie later, Chelsea grabbed my arm.

"Mark doesn't wear a watch," she whispered furiously.

"No? Okay, then, we move to the next course of action." We ducked into an alcove near the snack bar, where I could tell her about our breakfast plans without being overheard.

She threw her arms around me—again—and I laughed and patted her back. Only to see Mark standing behind us.

"Looks like someone has good news," he said.

Chelsea jumped away, startled, one hand flying to her gaping mouth. The way I saw it, we had what we wanted—his attention. And what was that line that celebrities used? Any publicity was good publicity?

"Oh, you know . . . ," Chelsea said, and her voice trailed off to no-man's-land.

He nodded. "Don't tell me. This is about Kate's date with Brandon tonight."

My jaw dropped.

"People were talking about it after school," he explained.

"Yeah," Chelsea said. "Pizza, right?"

All pretenses of covering for Chelsea or hooking the two of them up went out of my head. I just stood there, amazed at how people could be so in the know about the one aspect of my life I thought so little about.

"Yeah," I said, reaching deep inside myself for enough enthusiasm to sound sincere. "That's it. I'm so excited about tonight."

I should have won an Oscar for that one.

Five

Hours later, Brandon and I were working our way down my steep driveway. He moved with an athlete's grace, while my two-inch-spike-heeled boots proved a bit of a problem. Short black skirt plus high-heeled boots equaled Suzannah's idea of what to wear on a "date" with Brandon, not mine.

As soon as we settled into his car, he checked me out in the harsh dome light. "Two words: *way, way hot*."

That was three. But who was counting?

Besides, while most Franklin Pierce girls would have traded a year's worth of lip gloss to hear Brandon

Callister say that line, I was pretty positive it was just that—a line. "Thanks, but come on. I know we're only out tonight because your mother thought you should let me down easy."

"That's not true."

"She suggested tonight, didn't she?"

He shrugged. "Yeah, but for a mom, sometimes she has good ideas."

I also suspected the woman had dropped him on his head as a baby—how else could his behavior be explained?—but tonight *was* in my best interest, so I snapped shut my seat belt. And my mouth.

Rolling Hills didn't have a lot of restaurants, and if you wanted pizza, Mama's was *the* place to go. Hot, stretchy mozzarella, crispy crust—and on a Friday night, appearances by anyone who was anyone under twenty-one.

Mama herself showed us to a cozy circular booth in a dark corner of the restaurant. I had a strange feeling she'd been waiting.

Heads turned, people nodded and said our names. What was next? The flash of paparazzi's cameras?

The whole thing felt so public and awkward that for the first time since I could remember, I was speechless. Luckily, Brandon had never been short on words. So, breaking with our lab tradition, I sat back and let him talk. Anything to get through the date.

He talked about baseball, a cousin who was in physical therapy following a car accident, and his addiction to online role-playing games.

Somewhere between the arrivals of a pitcher of Coke and the dinner salads, I warmed to the idea that despite his idiot, slacker mentality, Brandon was actually a decent guy. Not someone I wanted to be attached to, but not exactly the dregs of society, either. And I had to admit it got pretty entertaining when he leaped to the subject of his ex.

"All Summer ever cared about was how people looked. Clothes and stuff. And I mean, how many colors can you paint your fingernails?" he asked, exasperated. "And you can only ignore a person's endless talking for so long, you know?"

Oh, I knew. That was how I'd ended up on this date.

He crammed some pizza into his mouth. I had to point to my nose and nod until he thought to use his napkin to wipe off the grease.

"That's what I like about you, babe," he said, and smiled. He still had a streak of grease on his cheek, but I could live with it. "You're different from Summer and those girls."

Yeah, the popular ones.

"You've got goals. You know what you want, and you won't let anyone stop you from getting it."

"Even you," I said, and then, realizing how rudely it came out, I laughed. "You know, in chem lab, when you won't stop talking to me."

He studied me for a long moment. Blood rushed to my face and I was suddenly so hot that if someone had sprayed me with water, I probably would have steamed.

"I guess I give you a hard time, huh? But you know I've only been playing with you, right? Having fun. And besides, I like to look at you."

He smiled. And instead of looking just plain goofy, the smile deepened, putting a little *zing* in his eyes.

In that moment, my world shifted. I realized that maybe—just maybe—I'd been deluding myself about his feelings for me. Maybe we weren't on this date because he got backed into it or was being Mr. Nice Guy, but because he wanted to be.

And it hit me. It was now or never, and there was only one way to find out.

"Brandon," I said, my throat dry despite all the soda I'd poured down it. "That's a great watch you're wearing. Is it new?"

"I got it for my birthday."

"It—it's really cool." I swallowed hard. "Can I take a look at it?"

He glanced down at his wrist, a frown crossing his brow. "You want to . . . see it?"

I managed a nod.

With my heart pounding all the way to my ears, I watched his arm stretch across the table toward me.

"Here," he said, offering his wrist.

Omigod.

He was into me.

The undisputed Head Honcho of Franklin Pierce High School *liked me* liked me, and here we were, on a *legitimate* date. Which everyone else had understood all along. Everyone but me. Which made me the undisputed Airhead of Franklin Pierce High School.

Luckily, Brandon launched into a tedious story about what he'd really wanted for his birthday, giving me time to think things through.

I told myself he surely wasn't all *that* into me. We barely knew each other and had nothing in common. It had to be a thrill-of-the-hunt thing for him. So if I went with my instinct to go to the bathroom and run out the back door, it would only make him want me more, right?

I had to sit tight.

After what felt like an eternity of nodding and polite listening, I reminded him that we needed to get the bill if we were going to make the movie. And sure enough, when the bill came, he refused to let me put in a cent.

Then, as we started making our way around the tables to leave, the unthinkable happened. He moved in close and draped a loose—but possessive—arm around me. Declaring our couple status to the fifty or so pairs of eyes in a move even louder than buying those banquet tickets from Carlton "The Mouth" Camp.

Horror, panic, and something else I couldn't even identify zipped through my bloodstream. I wanted to lift his wrist, watch and all, and hurl it like a ticking time bomb. *No way* I was becoming the Girlfriend of Brandon Callister.

"I—I think I left my cell phone on the table," I said, and ducked away from his hold. "I'll go check and meet you at the door."

He looked confused, but after a few seconds he re-sumed walking.

I was safe and free. For the moment.

The real drama came after the movie, when we were alone, parked outside my house. One second we were sitting on our own sides of the car, and the next he was using his athletic talent to lunge at me across the gearshift.

"Brandon," I said, shrinking away and grabbing the door handle. No more games, no more making nice. Time to get real. "You're a good guy. But I just don't *feel* for you what I think you want me to feel."

He stopped, pulling back. "You don't?"

His voice rose an entire octave, like he'd dropped about ten years, making me feel almost sorry for him. I mean, ever since he and Summer had split, he'd had his pick of girls. He probably had no coping mechanisms for rejection.

"Is there someone else, Kate?"

I shook my head.

"Then why . . ." His voice trailed off, then returned with renewed strength. "So if I were to ask you to wait for me, would you do that?"

Wait for him? What? Was I suddenly in a freaking romance novel?

"Kate," he went on, "there's no one like you in the whole school, who is so mature and smart and pretty. Being around you makes me feel so good. Give me one more date, one more try."

I studied his face. I had no idea what he was talking about. As far as I was concerned, I didn't stand out at school at all—and besides, there wasn't enough chemistry between us to fill a test tube. "Even if I said yes, Brandon, nothing between us would change."

"You don't know that."

"I do."

"Give me a chance. Wait for me. It's only for two weeks, and not like you've got anything else going on, right?"

"Well, no—"

"We'll be text and e-mail buddies."

I stared into his eyes. "You really want that?"

"Sure do. I'll leave here feeling great about things. I'll totally hit more homers, catch more fly balls, impress the coaches. Think of it as a good deed you're doing my career."

Oh, so *that* was it! It was one of those sports superstition things, like major leaguers who always ate the same meal before games. "So I'd be like your good-luck charm?"

"Sure. Okay?"

Hmmm . . . I didn't mind helping him get recruited—he deserved to play college baseball. And I had a suspicion that this little arrangement could be good for me, too. Keep my name on people's lips, maybe steer me toward some Ideal Opportunities?

"Oh, why not?" I said, and let out a laugh.

He grinned and lurched toward me—lips first.

"Brandon!" I ducked as fast as I could. I think he kissed my barrette.

"Just one?"

I cranked open the door and swung my legs out. "Don't push it."

He sighed, and before I could jump out, he grabbed a flyer from the floor, ripped it in half, and scribbled his cell number and e-mail address on it. The only thing I could do to get out of there was to jot down my info on the other half. When I handed it to him, he took my hand.

"I'll see you in two weeks, Kate."

But when I tried to take my hand back, he wouldn't let go. He just stared into my eyes like he'd been frozen.

"Yeah," I said. "And thanks for tonight." I yanked my hand free and scrambled out of the car, refusing to think about what I might have gotten myself into.

So what if I took myself off the market for two weeks? Who would even notice? I was just happy to get out of the car with all my limbs intact.

Six

I woke up the next day ready for business. The Brandon Thing was behind me—or at least out of my head for the time being—and I had a solid, income-generating venture to focus on.

Lexie's dad carted her to practices on weekends, thank God, so I had two whole days to myself. Though I'd never turn down extra billable hours, I'd had enough of the Rink Rat for the week.

I was looking forward to the breakfast meeting, to throwing my heart and soul into closing this deal.

Chelsea looked amazing when she slipped into my

passenger seat. She'd blow-dried her hair straight and shiny, and wore a body-hugging shirt that stopped just above her low-riding jeans. She'd topped it with a brown corduroy jacket, and her eyes were positively glowing from excitement and what I believe was a bit of shimmery eye shadow.

I couldn't wait for Mark to check her out. I could practically hear the *cha-ching* of the cash register.

The guys came through the door a few minutes after we did. Dal led Mark up and down the aisles until he spotted us. He turned and said something to Mark, then they moved to our table.

I knew what I had to do, what I had to say. It was all about staying calm.

"Kate!" Dal said. Which might have come off well, if not for the catch in his voice that stretched my name into two or three syllables.

The phoniness of the situation hit me like a Spokane cloudburst. I knew if I so much as opened my mouth, I'd laugh. So I did the only thing I could do—I drew a deep breath and held in all air and sound. Even though it meant totally blowing my part.

Chelsea spoke up. "Hey, Dal. And Mark."

The guys nodded hello to her.

Dal's gaze went bug-eyed as he glared at me. "So, Kate, it looks like you haven't ordered yet."

I knew if I couldn't get through this charade, I'd never get through a corporate interview. So I grabbed a napkin from the dispenser, brought it to my mouth, and coughed a little. "Uh, hey," I managed. "Why don't you guys join us?"

Dal wriggled in next to me before Mark had a chance to speak. Phase One, complete. Even if its key players had had a devil of a time delivering their lines.

But Dal was clearly in game mode, because as soon as Mark was in his seat, he turned and asked me if I was going to the football banquet. Though it was the perfect intro, I was kind of thrown by how quickly everything was happening.

Mark jumped in before I could answer. "I thought Brandon couldn't go, Kate. And that's why you two went out last night."

I just stared, not sure how to respond, how to get back on track.

Mark continued. "But I heard you had a great time, and that you're officially a couple now."

My hand went to my chest, fingers spread over my heart, just in case I had a coronary. "What? No! And where are you hearing all this?" Was someone blogging my life or something?

"From Vince Hammer," he said, referring to another baseball player. "We were IMing last night."

Holding Mark's gaze, I had this vision of myself innocently sleeping while IMs popped up all over Rolling Hills, broadcasting the millisecond when Brandon's arm had rested on my shoulder in Mama's.

I shook my head, trying to rid myself of that terrible thought. Then I felt Dal's eyes boring into the side of my head. I didn't owe him any more of an explanation than I did Mark or Chelsea—or anybody.

"We had an okay time. And we left it open-ended. We'll go out again when he gets back from his baseball thing, but we're definitely not 'together.' " I stared at Mark. "Did he say that?"

"No, but he didn't have to. He's into you."

"Yeah," Chelsea said. "You two are such a cute couple."

I rolled my eyes. Then I glanced at Dal, expecting radioactive waves of disapproval.

He just shrugged. Which, actually, bugged me. What, he no longer cared if I "threw my future away"? So I shifted until I was facing him. "What's your take?" I asked, point-blank.

Again, the full-shouldered shrug. "None of my business."

"It's everybody's business when you're with a guy like Brandon," Chelsea said, and giggled. "Everybody notices him. And what girl *wouldn't* go out with him?"

Her words hung in the air. I tried to come up with a smooth save, but my heart function must have affected my brain, because it suddenly felt short on blood and oxygen.

I used to be that girl who *wouldn't* go out with him— or at least would never have had to face the problem of debating the pros and cons of it.

But now I did. And I probably had to go out with him again. (What had I been thinking?)

Mark made a noise in the back of his throat and looked down at his menu. Which catapulted me back into business mode. I had a job to do—which I was failing miserably at. The beautiful girl sat next to the seemingly interested guy, but instead of focusing on him, she was gushing about someone else.

And Dal seemed to have thrown in the towel—or at least handed it off to me. I clearly had to take back control of this project.

A waitress with more boob than blouse came to take our order, but neither guy looked up long enough to even properly inspect her.

How would Donald Trump reestablish control? Start throwing money around? Steer the conversation to his advantage? Fire someone? Think, Kate!

And slowly it came to me. My copy of *Trump: The Art of the Deal* was more worn than my favorite jeans. He'd tell me to go with my instincts. And my instincts were to redirect the conversation to the banquet.

"So, Mark," I said, and waited for him to look at me. "Are *you* going to the football banquet?"

"Yeah, sure, I have to. I'm on the team."

I gave my head a firm nod, then turned to Chelsea. "Doesn't your brother play, too?"

"Yeah, on JV."

"Oh, do they have the same banquet?" I asked, as if I didn't know.

She nodded.

"Must be boring," I said. "You know, all those awards and stuff."

Chelsea finally got a clue and clicked into gear. "Yeah, at least where I sit. Back with the parents and little kids. It's probably more fun with the players and their dates. Isn't it, Mark?"

I turned and gave Dal a discreet, urgent look. "Excuse me," I said. "I need to use the restroom."

He slid out, letting me by. "I—I've gotta go, too," he said, finally getting with the program.

I don't think I took a decent breath until he and I rounded the corner. I paused by the door of the women's room and pulled Dal out of view. "This hookup thing is harder than I thought."

"No kidding."

I peeked around the corner, saw Mark talking and Chelsea smiling, and ducked back. "I just hope we pull this off."

"I think we might. I mean, did you see Mark's double take when he first saw her?"

I nodded, only a little bit lying. I *had* watched Mark's face light up for about three seconds. Before Dal's voice had caught and I'd completely lost my game.

"Now," Dal said, leaning against the wall, "if she'll just shut up about how every girl wants Brandon Callister, we should be fine."

I nodded.

"What's with Brandon, anyway? What does he have that the rest of us don't?"

"Not a thing."

"Oh, come on, Kate. If anybody knows, it's you." He smirked. "You *are* his girlfriend, after all, right?"

The way he drew out "girlfriend" told me he knew better. Still, I was sick and tired of the misconception. "I am *not*. We're not even dating. I mean, not *dating* dating."

"Define 'dating.' "

"More like seeing," I said.

"Seeing?"

"Well, not *seeing* seeing."

"Kate . . ."

"I'm waiting for him."

"Waiting," he repeated. "But not *waiting* waiting, right?"

"Right."

He exhaled loudly. "So, you're waiting for what?"

"One last date. So then we can go back to being just lab partners."

"Does he know this? You know, he's not the sharpest tool in the shed, and even I'm having trouble following this conversation."

"If he was paying attention last night, he knows." I couldn't resist playing myself up a bit, giving Dal the hard time he'd earned. What did I have to lose? "But Suzannah talked me into wearing my high-heeled boots and my short black skirt, so I probably blinded him with my mile-long legs."

"Your mile-long . . ." His voice trailed off. "Yeah, I

remember those legs. Attached to cement feet when they gracefully crashed into kids at the bottom of the playground slide."

Okay—not the response I wanted. But even when I was perturbed or annoyed or downright mad at Dal, he still managed to make me smile. Which I did. Darn him.

I peeked around the corner again. The waitress was delivering our omelets and pancakes, and Chelsea and Mark had stopped talking. Bad. But they hadn't stopped looking at each other. Good?

"Let's go back," I said. "See if it's time for a victory lap or more damage control."

By the time we were done eating and ready to head home, the sky had turned a steely gray and the temperature had plummeted. Chelsea and I sat in my car in the parking lot, blasting the heat until we saw the guys pull out into traffic. Then we squealed and hugged— and she did some sort of jumping-up-and-down-in-her-seat thing.

Mark and Chelsea were going to the banquet together.

Had the hookup been easy? No way.

Did I have a clue what I was doing? None.

Had I made mistakes? Absolutely.

But would I hold this success close to my heart, as a sign that I really *was* ready to roll up my sleeves and take on the business world? You know it!

I grinned practically the whole drive to Chelsea's, and made sure to compliment her outfit and hair one last time and to ask if she had special plans for her look on an everyday basis before the banquet.

She seemed taken aback. "I'll probably just keep blow-drying my hair," she said. "And I have a new sweater I might wear this week."

"Sounds good," I said, and nodded, hoping she was getting the underlying message that in situations like these, looks *did* count.

I dropped her off and drove the half mile to Dal's. I found him in his driveway, locking up his mom's van. I knew that their cracked asphalt needed repaving and that the house could use new siding and paint, but all I saw was Dal.

He had the hood up on his green parka and moved woodenly, like he was trying to retain body heat.

I powered down the window and handed him his closing cut, plus some singles. "We did it!"

"We did." He grinned, pocketed the tens, but thrust the singles back at me.

"Keep it," I told him. "I said I'd cover breakfast."

He folded the bills into my hand. I knew money was tight at his house, but if he wanted to give some back, well, who was I to argue?

"I wouldn't have missed that meal for anything, Kate. The tension, the forced conversation, the pancakes now sitting like a boulder in my stomach."

"It wasn't *that* bad. Sure, in the end, we had to

practically hit Mark over the head with the idea of asking her to the banquet, but he *did* get with the program."

A smile still lingered on his mouth.

"*And* we got paid," I added.

"Yeah. I made enough for a tank of gas to see Marissa."

Marissa again. *That* took the helium out of my balloon. "Now?" I asked. "I mean, you're going to see her today?"

"Probably next weekend," he said, and jammed his hands into his pockets. "I have to work later. And if it snows, the roads will be bad."

"Yeah." But it wasn't the impending weather that made me put the car back into gear. "Okay, I'm off. Have a good weekend if I don't see you."

He backed away toward the house and lifted a hand in a wave.

As I pulled onto the street, I smiled and returned his wave, but down deep I was more than a little bugged that I'd just bought Dal more Marissa time.

Seven

That night, around a lopsided homemade chocolate cake at the dining room table, Suzannah and I attempted some sisterly harmony.

". . . happy birthday, dear Daaaaad . . . happy birthday to *you*!"

Our end note was *so* flat that both Suz and I burst into laughter. Even Dad chuckled.

Still, I told myself we were throwing him a great little bash. Next would be presents and hunks of cake—which would hopefully taste better than it looked—followed by a board game of Risk that might go on for hours. Days, even. Who knew?

It was the perfect celebration inside the perfect home with the perfect family who was perfectly happy.

Father, daughter, and daughter.

No one else was invited (or missed). Especially not a certain someone who hadn't been home since Thanksgiving. Who had told us, in a no-nonsense, you-should-be-mature-enough-to-understand tone, that Christmas was too close to the semester end to be away from classes. And that Easter would be here "before you know it."

Whatever. Besides, I'd spent seventeen years in the presence of that woman. I'd done my time.

Back before she got the diploma bug, I *had* rather liked her. I'd thought she was sweet and fun and pretty—and way better than the mothers who obsessed about refined sugar and violence on TV.

Pam DelVecchio had always been different. For one thing, she was much younger than other mothers. She and Dad had met in high school. My sister and I were both born before my parents could even order a beer.

Instead of carrying a purse or diaper bag, my mom always seemed to have a book. Not a paperback, but a big, honking textbook on whatever serious subject she was studying. We grew up with her telling us about her courses, sometimes reading passages aloud while we played. I don't remember understanding much of it, but it didn't matter. I just liked to hear her voice.

By the time I was in middle school, my mother had a couple of BAs and had moved on to grad school. And sure enough, one master's degree wasn't enough. She went for a second, and was considering a third when she learned about a particular PhD program in Frankfurt, Germany.

Her persistent interest didn't surprise me. It was the timing I didn't buy. Was my mother running to this European program—or running from us?

Dad was blowing out his candles when the telephone rang. We all knew who it was. Suzannah, dropping about five of her years, let out a little-kid squeal and skated across the room for the cordless.

I felt a frown etch itself into my forehead, one angry line at a time.

"Hi, Mom!" Suz yelled, loud enough for us and all of Germany to hear, grinning like an idiot.

Suz actually bought the parents' spiel. That this PhD program was a once-in-a-lifetime opportunity for Mom, and that she would be back for good next summer. That they didn't want to wrench us from our friends—especially me from my senior year—and that space between mother and daughters in the teen years was a good thing, anyway.

But I was sure there was way more to this other-side-of-the-world thing than they were telling us.

"Put her on the speakerphone," Dad instructed.

And as soon as my mom's voice hit the air, he smiled, too.

Not me, though. Long gone were the days when her thoughts and her read-alouds filled me with warmth and a sense of security.

Suz and Dad did most of the talking on our end. Then, finally, my mother turned the bright light on me.

"I haven't heard much from you, Kate. And you didn't answer my last e-mail."

I studied my sneakers, feeling like an employee who hadn't made her sales quota. "Yeah, well . . ."

"She's been busy," my sister jumped in. "With her new boyfriend, Brandon Callister."

I rolled my eyes.

"What's this?" my mother said, although her voice showed no emotion.

I paused, wondering how to best spin Brandon. While our mother encouraged Suzannah and me to date and have fun, she'd warned us a gazillion times about getting serious. You know, to protect us from following the dead-ended, miserable early marriage path she had chosen.

"He's *so* gorgeous, Mom," Suz answered for me. "You should see him."

"Wow," Mom simply said. But caution edged her words. "What do *you* think, Kate?"

I was tempted to tell her that Brandon and I were mad for each other's bods and were already secretly engaged. Just to see what she'd say. But my life was "complikated" enough without my mother's big, long-distance nose in it.

Despite my urge to freak my mom out, I went with the truth. "He's overrated. And we're not really going out, anyway. He's just my lab partner."

Suzannah let out this dramatic sigh—for our mother's benefit, I was sure—and announced she'd take Brandon off my hands whenever I was done with him.

"Ha! That's Kate's call," our mother responded emotionlessly.

Urg! And since it seemed I couldn't win on the subject of Brandon with anyone, I changed topics.

"I made some extra money this week," I said after clearing my throat. "Helping a girl from the rink." I held my head a little bit higher. "Bringing me closer to what I'm going to need at graduation."

In other words . . . *There, lady!* See, I *am* going to make my goal, get that college money, and do things my way. You're not the only one who can call the shots.

"Really?" our mother responded, noncommittal. "How was that?"

"Matchmaking," my dad offered.

Huh? I shot a look at him and then turned to Suzannah, who gave me a guilty shrug.

"Matchmaking?" my mother repeated, then laughed.

I exhaled. First of all, it wasn't matchmaking. I'd read an article about those ladies. Mostly older women, they took their business very seriously, researching suitable mates for their unmarried clients and introducing them over tea or something.

What I'd done was embark on a covert mission, like James Bond. Okay, maybe more like Austin Powers. Or like Will Smith in that movie *Hitch.* But still, I'd treated it like I would any business venture, with seriousness, flexibility, and multiple points of contact, and I'd even outsourced some of the work to a top-notch contractor. Best of all, I'd succeeded.

And the fact that my mother was laughing . . . well, I'd get that five thousand dollars if I had to wade through sewers for pennies. Okay—yuck. If I had to take Lexie to that New York City qualifying competition myself. Actually not such a bad idea.

"I'm surprised that little scheme didn't blow up in your face, Kate," my mother said. "Didn't I tell you not to mess with affairs of the heart?"

No, Mother Dearest, I must have missed that lecture while you were showing me how to grocery shop and vacuum under the couch and all the other duties you should be here doing.

"Well, I did just fine," I answered, and braced myself for a slam.

But it didn't come. In fact, her voice took on some warmth. "I'm glad, honey. And . . . you know I'm proud of you. After you get the right degrees, the Fortune Five Hundred companies are going to be breaking their necks trying to get you."

The right degrees! She *still* wasn't hearing me about how I wasn't going to do things her way.

I felt the blood rushing to my face. And who was she to tell me what to do, a woman who wasn't even here to make her husband his birthday cake?

Dad shot me a warning look.

Suzannah shook her head.

So I took a deep breath and gave my mother a dose of her own medicine. I laughed.

The party wasn't quite the same after that. We did presents and cake, but then Dad wanted to go watch TV. Suz called a friend, and I ended up in my room, surfing the Web.

I couldn't concentrate on anything, and eventually I fell asleep on top of my bedspread. At some point, I kicked off my sneakers and crawled under the covers. And at another, I woke to the sound of my IM message chime. I ignored it and rolled over.

In the morning, I wasn't sure if I'd dreamed the pesky IM chimes or imagined them in a falling-asleep hallucination. But as I climbed out of bed, I squinted at my laptop to see if I had a waiting message. And sure enough, the text box was open on my screen, and there was a message from SPEEDBALL:

u there?
cant believe Im going 2 tryouts 2morrow
cant sleep.

And then another:

kate?????

A shiver ran down my spine. Brandon, feeling anxious? Brandon, wanting to talk about his feelings?
With me?

This was a whole new animal from the guy I knew in
chem lab. One I didn't particularly *want* to know. It felt
too . . . personal. Too connected. And what could *I*
possibly say to help?

Just as well that I'd kept sleeping.

Eight

I snagged a premium space in the senior lot when I got to school. It was on an end, which cut the risk of getting dinged, and I took it as a sign that the day would go my way. Good thing, because I had an essay test that could have been the death of my A, and after school I had my bimonthly Future Business Leaders meeting.

Suzannah was leaning against the car, trying to stuff a lunch sack in a too-full compartment of her backpack, when a shrill female voice rang out from the next lane.

"There she is!"

I reached to help Suz with the bulging zipper, not bothering to look up. Sorry to say, but neither of us had ever achieved that level of *she*-dom.

But the voice grew louder. "Hey!" That was followed by the sudden rush of footsteps. "Hey, Kate!" that same high-pitched voice called out.

I glanced over to see four girls heading straight for us, smiles plastered across their faces. I'd been in classes with all of them at one time or another, but the only name that stuck in my head was Aimee McDonald, who was the ringleader.

Aimee was one of those people whose skin was so pale it was almost translucent. But since she exuded such a supernatural sense of self-confidence, you pretty much looked past her washed-out complexion to her dazzling blue eyes and dynamic aura.

Chewing gum and smiling at the same time—which was gross, take my word for it—she stopped in front of me. "*So . . . ,*" she said, like we talked every day. "How's our guy doing?"

I was tempted to ask, "Who?" But I wasn't a fool—even if I wasn't a girlfriend, either. "Fine, I guess."

She looked as shocked as if I'd said diet soda had been banned from the campus. "You *guess*? You haven't heard from him?"

Truth was, I couldn't be bothered to respond to the IMs he'd sent and I'd turned off my laptop. I wouldn't boot it up again until this afternoon at the rink.

My sister must have read my mind, because she

pushed ahead of me. "Brandon probably left her a hundred messages. She'll find out when she gets around to checking."

Aimee's palm went to her cheek in one of those clichéd gestures. "You haven't checked them since he's been gone?"

"Not really," I admitted.

"Omigod." She laughed, then shook a finger. "You are *so* bad, Kate!"

I just stared at her. What was I supposed to say? Sorry? Or explain for the hundredth time that I was not Brandon's girlfriend?

"Actually, she's smart," my sister piped up. "While half the girls at school were throwing themselves at him, she was sitting back, playing it cool. Now she's got him. So why change what's working?"

Surprised, I turned to Suz. For someone who could be so blind about what was going on in our home life, she was killer on these defensive comebacks. I might have to hire her to do my PR someday.

Aimee smacked her gum. "Try checking your e-mails on a class computer. And go off campus during morning break and turn on your phone. Then come by our table at lunch and give us the absolute latest, okay?"

I nodded, although I knew I'd do nothing of the sort. And where *was* their table, anyway?

"Remember, us first, okay?" she said, then threw her arms around me.

I nearly gagged on her bubble gum scent.

"We're so happy for you, Kate," a husky-voiced girl added, and almost sounded sincere.

"I mean, okay," Aimee said, pulling back from me. "*Some* of us wouldn't have minded getting our hands on Brandon Callister ourselves." She laughed, a little too loudly. "But you got him fair and square. Playing hard to get or whatever. Plus people say you've got some get-rich-quick scheme that's going to make you a millionaire, like, tomorrow. How could he *not* love that?"

"Well," I said, suddenly on more comfortable ground. "It's more like a plan. And it'll be a few years, for sure."

"Whatever." She patted my arm, as if I'd been tried and found worthy of being Queen to His Royal Hotness. "So . . . later, right?" She turned away, and her friends fell in behind her.

Mrs. Quack and all her little ducklings.

I just stared. Then I leaned toward my sister. "What," I asked, "was that?"

Suz rested her head on my shoulder. "I don't know how to tell you this, Kate. But I think you're popular."

In the halls, people I barely knew nodded at me. Those I did know flashed smiles. Some said my name.

I wondered if Katie Holmes had gone through something like this when she'd first hooked up with Tom Cruise.

Arriving at my locker, I found my locker-mate,

Yvette DelaCruz, holding court with a few girls. She and I had been sort-of friends since elementary school, even though she was one of the most hyper people I'd ever met. Not in a needs-meds kind of way, but in a needs-a-life kind of way. Yvette got totally pumped up at school and was forever moving, whether it was doing a pretzel-twist thing with her legs or gesticulating wildly with her hands. I swear, she was like a performance artist.

"Hey," I said as I walked up to her squirming body.

Yvette stopped moving. Completely. She and her friends turned toward me and said hello. Her stillness was unnerving.

I managed a smile, then threw some books onto my shelf.

"Where is he now?" Yvette asked. Once again, the identity of "he" being implied.

I was frozen in place by her calmness and had to think for a few seconds before I could answer. "Arizona."

"I know that, *silly*. Where in Arizona?"

How in the world would I know? Sure, he'd told me some details over dinner, but my head had been spinning from having Mama herself seat us, and from seeing all the craned necks and stares. Plus—who really cared?

"I'll have to get back to you on that," I said, reverting to a safe, businesslike tone. Then I nodded a quick goodbye.

Yvette turned back to her friends, and I heard her say, "She'll keep us posted."

As I blended into the passing crowd, people kept nodding at me, smiling, and saying my name. I didn't want to be rude, so I formed something like a smile on my face and shot it like a laser at everyone in my path.

Dakota Watson was standing in the doorway of my classroom and brightened up when she saw me. I guess she didn't think I looked like a dog *this* morning, either.

"Well, well, Miss Thing," she said, and did this so-fast-you-barely-saw-it swoop of her long, dark hair so it hung to one side of her neck like a dark scarf. "I hope you're proud of yourself."

I kept myself in check, didn't act surprised that she was lowering herself to speak to me, or bring up Friday's too-loud commentary. "And I hope you're ready for the meeting later, Dakota. You're reporting on hot trends, right?"

She put a manicured nail in her mouth. One thing about Dakota—her shiny-haired beauty wasn't enough. She always went the extra mile with cosmetics and clothing.

"I'm surprised you had time to remember, DelVecchio, after the weekend you had. But yeah, I'm totally ready." She leaned in, like we were BFFs. "And actually, after the meeting, I'd like to talk to you."

"Sorry," I said, a little flattered, a little curious. "But I'm *so* out of here afterwards. Have to get the Hoppenfeffer kid to practice. What's up?"

She puckered her pinker-than-pink lips. "Nothing I want to talk about here. Maybe I'll call you tonight."

I shrugged and moved on by, happy for once to go into history class and lose myself in other people's lives.

I spent lunch with Dal. We munched on soft tacos from the food truck and talked about everything and nothing, but one thing was distinctly different about the day. People kept stopping by to congratulate me and to ask about Brandon. I answered their questions but sensed that Dal was getting as annoyed as I was.

After lunch, a short girl was waiting by my locker. I was tempted to offer her my autograph if she'd go away.

A closer look and I recognized her from Suzannah's grade, probably from some school project committee Suz had once worked on. As I noted her French braid and cupid's-bow mouth, "cute" was the word that came to mind.

"Hi, Kate," she greeted me as I walked up. "I'm Vince's sister. Jenn."

Ah, yes, Baseball Vince, who'd IM'd Mark with the news that Brandon and I were a couple. My, my, how small Franklin Pierce really was.

"Have you heard from Brandon?" she asked.

I shook my head.

"Well, I've got a message for him." She went on to give me some story about a DVD that Brandon had left at their house, and how some friend wanted to borrow it, and was that okay.

It was enough I'd been labeled his girlfriend—now I was his secretary, too? But I swallowed my irritation. I was, after all, a cooperative person. His e-mail address was pretty much the same as his IM, so it was easy for me to remember. I figured she could just give him the message herself, so I rattled it off to her.

Then, before I could say bye, Chelsea suddenly replaced Vince's sister in front of me, wearing makeup and a great pair of earrings.

"Mark smiled at me twice in the hall," she said, and did a dreamy eye roll. "And came and sat with me for a few minutes at lunch. Kate, I could just die!"

It wasn't every day I made someone happy. And it was almost *never* that I helped send someone over the moon. It was weird, but I really did feel warm inside. "Don't die, Chelsea," I said, and laughed. "At least not until after the banquet. I worked too hard."

Her grin widened.

In fifth period, a couple of girls got out of their seats to come and talk to me. But my sixth period was much calmer, which kind of surprised and disappointed me. (Oh, how quickly fame goes to one's head!)

Walking to my Business Leaders meeting after school, I thought about the accomplishments portion, when members mentioned their successes, and wished I could announce how I'd hooked up Chelsea and Mark. Closing that deal had required many of the strategies we discussed in meetings. But it had also required confidentiality.

I could hear club members' voices filtering down the hall. One thing I'd learned about budding entrepreneurs: we liked to talk. About ourselves and those we admired. And often all at once. So despite my best efforts, most meetings ran like water through my fingers. I just hoped today's didn't.

The noises got louder as I pulled open the classroom door. The usual twelve or fifteen people were milling in small groups around the classroom. Mr. Packard sat at his desk, beneath a few of his favorite motivational posters.

I dropped my backpack in a corner and nodded hello to him, then moved to his podium. I grabbed hold of the gavel and gave it a couple of hard bangs.

What happened next stunned me. Delighted me. Reminded me that this day was like no other in my entire life.

All heads turned my way. And the voices died. I mean, there was a huge possibility you could have heard a pin drop.

"I am calling this meeting of the Future Business Leaders of America to order," I said, and watched the most driven, hardheaded group of people in the school slip obediently into their seats.

Life was good!

I got through announcements and new business in record time. No interruptions, no arguments, no paper airplanes to duck. Then Dakota stood up and gave her hot trends talk on the effect of interest rates on the current real estate market.

While she spoke, I studied people's expressions, tried to read their eyes. Girls like Aimee McDonald might go giggle crazy over Brandon (and by association, me), but *these* were the movers and shakers. Honor students, student government reps, the ones most likely to get into Ivy League schools and armed services academies.

I knew they respected my Millionaire Before Twenty plan, even though none of them had the guts to jump feetfirst into the business world yet themselves. So why would my supposedly dating a jock increase their respect for me? *What* was I missing?

"I just want to end this with a special thank-you to our club president," Dakota said, shooting a grin at me. "For all the hard work she does for us."

The members broke into applause. Jon Keller—who ever since losing the senior class president bid to a girl with purple hair had been far more prone to put-downs than compliments—even got to his feet.

I just didn't get it.

I glanced over at Mr. Packard, but he seemed engrossed in correcting papers.

Red-faced, I walked back up to the podium, but I couldn't keep up the ruse any longer. "I take it you guys are referring to my new friendship with Brandon—"

A voice rang out from the back of the room, the first

sign of normalcy we'd had all meeting. "Forget him! Tell us about your Six-Point Plan!"

"Yeah," called out Gracie, who summered as an intern at our congressman's office. "Your *secret* formula that's going to make you rich."

My lips parted, and my fingers raced to the neckline of my T-shirt.

"And make us rich, too!" someone else shouted.

Okay, this was *worse* than a naked dream. This was one of those terror dreams where you need to scream, need to run, but you're frozen. You simply have to stand there and take it.

How could they have heard about my Six-Point Plan? (Not that it even existed.) Who had I even mentioned it to? Chelsea, to be sure. My sister? Dal?

"That's confidential," I managed to reply.

"Come on," Jon shouted. "There's money enough out there for all of us. Spill the beans!"

I swallowed, several times. "I—I don't know what you're talking about. Now, moving along to our next—"

Jon jumped up. "If you're not going to share it, then I'm outta here. I've got things to do."

Gracie stood. "Me too." She turned and started talking to someone across the room about homework.

Another guy put his sweatshirt hood up.

Dakota sighed loudly and rolled her eyes.

Questions raced through my head. How did they know about my Six-Point Plan? How did I regain order? How could I get them to listen to me again, to respect me?

"Everybody," I said. But nobody looked. "Hey, people!"

Again, nothing.

Oh, the heck with it—I had better things to do with my time, too. "I hereby declare this meeting adjourned," I said, and banged the gavel so hard I thought the wood might splinter.

Nine

Somewhere between school, the Hoppenfeffers' house, and Winter Wonderland, my emotions took a backseat to my thoughts. I asked myself honestly why I had gotten so upset at the meeting.

Inside the rink, I followed Lexie to her team bench, where she plopped down between a couple of girls and got to work tying her laces. I saw that her right lace was shredded—we'd *talked* about this last week, she was supposed to tell her mom—and instead of my usual do-it-yourself attitude, I moved over, went down on one knee, and took over the tying of her rainbow-colored lace myself. I didn't want it coming untied and tripping her during practice. I would for sure be the one blamed.

Moments later, her laces tied tightly, Lexie took to the ice. I had to admit the kid had style. Speed. Talent. It was amazing that she'd only been skating a few years. Most of the other girls had started by kindergarten, and she was as good as any of them, if not better.

But Lexie did have an advantage. Her dad could skate. I mean, *really* skate. Rocko Hoppenfeffer had been one of those Venice Beach, California, surfer dudes who'd apparently reinvented the skateboarding wheel back in their day. He'd made serious money doing skateboard endorsements, and instead of (or maybe in addition to?) wasting it on partying and girls he'd invested it up here in land and paper mills, making himself pretty appealing to the town's local celebrity, our also successful and slightly eccentric romance writer. A few years later, they'd had Lexie, who they seemed to like a lot more than I did, so I guess they were living happily ever after.

On the occasions I thought about Lexie's natural abilities on the ice, I wondered if her love for skating got passed down through her DNA or if her über-talent came from an über-desire to please her dad.

Though if Lexie was only trying to please her dad, some could mistakenly say that my Millionaire Before Twenty plan was just an attempt to get pats on the back from my overachieving mother.

And that couldn't have been farther from the truth.

Up in my office, I'd barely had time to read the three texts and four e-mails from Brandon when feet rumbled up the bleachers.

I looked up to see Chelsea and Dakota. And while these two seemed about as likely a pair as tartar sauce and a hot dog, suddenly the events at the meeting made sense. Chelsea and Dakota were friends. Chelsea must have blabbed to Dakota about my hooking her up with Mark. Dakota, in turn, had shared the details of my Six-Point Plan with the club before my arrival. Bingo! Mystery solved.

I closed my laptop and greeted them like we had this little get-together every day. Chelsea, her newly brushed and styled hair shining in the fluorescent light, stayed only long enough to say hi. Then Dakota plopped herself down next to me.

"I thought we could talk now."

I shrugged.

"The Six-Point Plan," she said. "Spill it. Before I lay down a penny, DelVecchio, I've got to know what I'm getting into."

Wait. Lay down a penny? Was she another potential customer? Was more capital coming my way?

I forced a poker face—even though it almost killed me—and slowly I explained what I'd do for her. "After I crunch the numbers and decide if the hookup is possible, that is," I added.

She inhaled, long and hard. "I want to see this hexagon."

Me and my big mouth.

I must have looked as hesitant as I felt, because she arched a brow. "I'm a Future Business Leader, too, and you owe it to me to be on the level. Besides, I've got connections. I happen to know at least two other people who'd also be willing to sign up for this. But *only* with my endorsement."

Two more? She had my interest, no doubt about it. And come on, how hard would it be to BS a Six-Point Plan? Harder than pulling off all As this semester and rounding up five thousand big ones to satisfy my parents? I think not!

"Okay, meet me at my locker before lunch tomorrow." I studied her face. "You going to tell me who the guy is?"

"After I see your hexagon."

"Okay, but I've got to warn you. It can't be somebody's boyfriend. The hexagon doesn't work with unavailable guys. I'm not out to break up couples."

"Yeah, yeah," she said, waving my warning away. "Chelsea already warned me that you won't help me get Dal."

I felt myself tighten. "You're after Dal?"

"No, I'm just saying."

"Okay, because he's taken."

She nodded, "So tomorrow for the Six-Point Plan?"

"Totally," I said. I had quite a night ahead of me.

That evening I sat in my room trying to come up with a Six-Point Plan that made any sense. Between

Internet sites, some of my sister's fashion magazines, and a girl's guide to manners that my mother had chucked at me eons ago, back when she had some herself, I made lists:

What girls looked for in guys.

What guys looked for in girls.

Basic turn-ons.

Basic turnoffs.

Statistics and information on what made a happy couple.

Tests to tell if a guy/girl liked you.

Interesting stuff, actually. But the bottom line in almost every article was honesty, and the golden rule seemed to be "just be yourself." Which was probably good advice for most people, but look where it had gotten me. People thought I was the girlfriend of a guy I could barely stand. And the only thing that had gotten me into that situation was just being myself. So you wouldn't see *me* preaching that stuff.

I tapped my nails on the keyboard, waiting for divine inspiration, and then it hit me. Or rather, it slowly sank in that I'd have to approach this problem like I did pretty much everything else in my life—by putting one foot in front of the other, armed with Wite-Out, an eraser, and the Delete key on my trusty laptop.

A half hour later, I pushed Save, then Print, which sent the document to the family computer setup down the hall. And none too soon, I held my future in my hot little hand.

Kate DelVecchio's Six-Point Plan
A Hexagon for Hooking Hotties

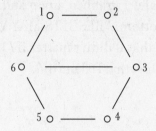

Above are six numbered points. Write the names of the potential couple on the center line. Read the questions. For every YES answer, darken the corresponding numbered point with a colored marker.

1: Are both parties unattached and available?

2: Do they have similar interests?

3: Are they on speaking terms?

4: Will they look good together?

5: Do they have a meeting ground outside of school (e.g., work, youth group, mutual friends' homes)?

6: Will their personalities click?

Once you have finished answering the questions and coloring the dots, connect all adjacent colored points with lines. When you are finished, examine your diagram. Is it a perfect hexagon for a perfect couple?

Flopping on my bed, I wasn't sure whether to be proud of myself or embarrassed. I mean, did the math terms make me look scholarly or like some little kid who used big words before she knew what they meant?

Just to be safe, I grabbed a pen and added in bold letters at the bottom: "RESULTS MAY VARY." And reminded myself that it didn't matter if *I* bought into the presentation. Only that Dakota did.

Ten

"What good does *this* do me?" Dakota screamed the next day, stabbing a finger at my printed hexagon. We'd snagged a couple of seats in Mr. Packard's empty classroom under the guise of working on club business, and until this moment, we had been munching somewhat pleasantly from our respective lunch sacks.

"*These,*" she continued, "are just questions."

No way was I letting her attitude get to me. I'd worked *hard* on the darned thing. I kept my eyes on the prize: her money. "It's the first step to determine whether or not I take you on as a client. Our preliminary interview, you might say."

"But I want specifics. A game plan."

"If I told you, what would be the point of hiring me? I mean, does KFC give out their secret recipe when people ask?"

I sort of held my breath while she made another grab for my hexagon. True, she held it like a used tissue—someone else's used tissue—but she studied it for a long moment nonetheless. "Okay," she said, and blew out on a sigh. "It's Jon. Jon Keller."

I steeled myself from letting my "eeewwww" show. Why she'd want to hang with someone so loud and negative was beyond me.

But hello! He was her mirror image. And that could mean either a supereasy hookup—or a supersized disaster.

The real question was why she wanted help from *me*.

"You know Jon as well as I do," I pointed out. "And I've never seen you let anything stand in the way of what you want. Why not just go directly to him?"

"I am looking at this like I would a business merger," she said matter-of-factly. "I want to create the right buzz, make him realize this partnership would be mutually beneficial, and that together our possibilities are endless." She flipped her hair to her other shoulder. "In short? I'm tired of two-week boyfriends. I want a relationship."

Whoa. Okay.

I dug up a red Sharpie from my backpack. The hexagon was about as accurate as a TV weather forecast, but what could I do?

"Are both parties unattached and available?" I read, trying not to smile. Like anyone but Dakota would want Jon. I darkened the point. "Similar interests?" I said, then marked it. In my book, being loud and arrogant counted as an interest.

"And we're definitely on speaking terms," she said, leaning in and jumping anxiously to the next question. "And—and we'll look good together."

Her opinion, but I went with it.

Then I hit an unknown and looked up. "Do you cross paths outside of school?"

Her brow knitted, which I took as a no.

"Have the same favorite hangout? Same friends? Same . . . I don't know . . . church or synagogue?"

"No." Worry flickered in her eyes. "Does that mean you won't take us on?"

I bit back a smile. My hexagon might have been based on nonsense, but it had successfully given me a shift of power, so it had done its job—and more. Plus, if I suspended reality long enough to assume it had some merit, it told me that this hookup needed to happen on campus, to take advantage of something they *did* have in common—our business club.

"Well . . . ," I said, suddenly having a little too much fun. "I might be able to take a five-out-of-sixer like you, but of course, it would cost extra." I paused, and when she didn't balk, I pushed on. "Hmmm . . . I'll need some additional information." My mind raced until it settled on one of those gems of the Internet: a does-he-like-me? test. "Do you two have any classes together?"

She nodded readily. "Next period."

I leaned in like I had to keep what I was about to say quiet. Even though we were alone I knew it all had to do with my delivery. I whispered instructions in her ear, then stood and stretched.

"Find me later, and we'll see if we can take this to the next step."

Her face twisted in desperation, making me want to break into a dance. I *so* had her!

After school, I arrived back at my locker to find an actual line. Like I was giving away free cell phone minutes or SAT cheat sheets.

Mark was there, sighing. Dakota was beside him, throwing her hair from one shoulder to the other, as usual. She was followed by a paper-thin girl in low-rider jeans. And Carlton Camp, from the student store. Thinking back to that day on the quad, I shouldn't have been surprised that he had a crush.

"I'm first," Dakota told the others in a don't-challenge-me tone.

"No," Mark said firmly. "I was here first. And my business with Kate is private." He eyed me seriously and nodded toward the row of lockers across the hall.

We took a few steps into traffic. I wanted this to be quick. I had some potential paying customers waiting, and although Mark didn't know it, his case was closed. "Can't whatever this is wait until the rink later?"

He shook his head. "One question." His face looked set—clamped mouth, fixed eyes. "Did Chelsea pay you to get me to ask her to the banquet?"

"What?" I said, freezing in place.

"You heard me."

My stomach clenched, and the world sort of went wavy before my eyes, like I was looking through my sister's glasses.

Mark knew. The Hook-ee had found out about the Hook-Upper. And he wasn't happy.

People streamed by us in both directions, their voices bouncing off lockers and the low-tiled ceiling, competing with the sudden rush of blood in my ears.

"That's . . . ," I finally said, and swallowed. ". . . confidential."

A curse fell from his mouth. I knew he had his answer. He turned away.

"Mark," I said, grabbing his arm. I waited until he met my gaze again. "Let's talk more about this. There's an explanation." At least, there would be, as soon as I came up with one.

"I thought we couldn't talk about it. That it was *confidential*." He turned up the intensity of his glare and pulled out of my grip.

It was my turn to mutter a curse.

Immediately, Dakota was on top of me. "He looked at the clock. Jon looked." A smile touched her mouth. "So we're on, right?"

It took me a second to regroup and remember the test I'd given her. The "Is He Staring at Me in Class?" test. The idea was for her to watch Jon out of the corner of her eye during class until she was pretty sure he was looking at her, then to throw an urgent look at the clock, hold a beat, and really fast, look back at him. If he was looking at the clock, odds were he'd followed her gaze. Which meant—bingo!—he'd been checking her out.

"That's good," I managed to tell her. "Real good. What we wanted." I drew in a breath. I really wanted to run this Dakota/Jon hookup by Dal first, to get his take. But odds were he'd be up for the challenge and the bucks, and it was best to strike while the iron was hot, right? "Okay, as soon as you deliver the deposit, we'll get to work."

She reached into her pocket and slipped me what looked like a folded-up note. But the paper had weight, and my superior senses could smell the U.S. currency.

"Call me tonight," she said, and left me to my line.

Before I could say bye to Dakota, Skinny Girl approached me. "How much?" the girl whispered.

"For what?" I had to make sure she wasn't expecting something bootlegged or illegal.

"You know, how much for you to hook me up with someone?" she said in that same superlow, hurried tone. Like she was afraid of getting caught.

I held her gaze. If this girl, who I didn't even know, knew about the business, word was truly out there. Which meant the discreetness I had been able to offer was now gone. I'd have to think that through, and use it to the best of my ability.

"Fifty up front, nonrefundable. And another fifty if we seal the deal."

She listened, lines forming in her brow, then backed away. "I don't have that kind of money," she said, loud enough for anyone near to hear.

"I'm sorry. But if I cut my rate for you, my other customers could demand the same. And I have expenses to cover." To keep her from asking for specifics on those expenses, which I couldn't exactly provide, I changed the subject. "By the way, how did you hear about me?"

A smile lifted her mouth. She was attractive, in an anemic sort of way. She'd probably be an easy fix-up. Maybe we could do some sort of installment plan.

"Who hasn't heard about you? You hooked Brandon Callister, you got Chelsea Mead a date with a football player. You're like . . . a love goddess."

Love goddess? No. Although how could I not like the sound of that?

But before I could respond, she disappeared into the crowd.

Carlton was instantly upon me. His bright blue eyes narrowed in on me like a laser beam, and my palm was suddenly holding some folded bills. I knew cash when I felt it. Still, I peeked. (I had to.) Tens and twenties. This guy did his homework.

"Brianne Betts," he said, the name floating on a long sigh.

I knew her. Big lips. Possibly collagen. Or maybe she had an ancestor who'd mated with a duck. No guarantees, but I'd give the two of them a try. "Sure, let's do it," I told him.

I slipped the wad of bills into the back pocket of my jeans. I felt rather like a human vending machine. Insert money, make your selection, and voilà, I will spit out your date! (Yeah, right.)

Carlton and I exchanged contact information. Then, finally alone—or as alone as anyone could be at my school—I did a book swap while I tried to make sense of everything that had just happened. I was torn between the euphoric feeling of having two more clients—and two more deposits—and well, guilt. Mark's anger was a shocker, and I had been completely and utterly unprepared for it.

Lots of thoughts. Lots of questions.

Only one answer: find Dal.

Eleven

Lexie wasn't ready when I got to her house, which meant I was forced to wait on the doorstep with her mother. I figured it was as good a chance as any to show Mrs. H. that I was a top-notch employee.

"Lexie's coach reminded everybody that deposits are due for the qualifying competition. I don't know if you paid already, but I thought I'd mention that if you or Mr. H. are unable to make the trip in May, I *will* be eighteen by then, and legally able to chaperone."

Mrs. H.'s gaze iced me. I shivered inside my coat— nothing to do with the freezing temperature.

"Just an FYI," I added.

She let out something like a snort. I figured I'd better get back on more solid ground, so I mentioned Lexie's broken laces and waited for her to tell me she had already bought twelve new fashion pairs or something.

"If you think it's so important," she answered, "pick her up some new ones yourself. I'll throw you a few extra dollars next payday."

My brow furrowed. They sold some plain old white laces at the rink. But those were hardly up to the elevated standard of what the other girls wore.

"Mom," Lexie said, cruising through the door. "New *laces*, remember? Did you buy them?"

I glanced at Mrs. H. Surely she'd take credit for assigning me the job. Instead, she shrugged. "Kate's taking care of it."

Then before either of us could respond, Mrs. H. closed the door—practically on Lexie's heels.

Wow.

As if nothing out of the ordinary had just happened, Lexie started toward my car. "I don't *like* the stupid ones they sell at the rink," she yelled back. "They're ugly."

"Yeah, well, if we stop anywhere, we'll be late. And we don't want penalty laps."

I felt a little bad for her. Her mom had practically shoved her out the door. But then she made a face at me, and I did the only thing I *could* do. I ignored it.

Dal stood behind the rental counter, shoving pairs of rental skates into cubbyholes, his triceps flexing with each haul.

I'd seen his arms plenty of times, and when I thought about them at all . . . well, I really didn't. Most days, I just looked away. But today, it was like someone had pushed my Pause button. I could only attribute their recent developments to all his hours with a hockey stick.

"Hey," he said, turning toward me.

I shook myself from my musing. My brain must have totally been on overload. Why else would I ever have looked at Dal's arms like . . . well, a hot guy's?

"A pair of your finest white laces, if you please," I said, and smiled big. "Size seventh grade annoying."

Amusement flickered in his eyes as he reached under the counter and slid a pair toward me. I passed him a ten and watched him count back my change.

"I'm not sure if you know, but we have a bit of a situation," he said as I pocketed the bills.

"Mark."

"Yeah. He was by here earlier. Pretty ticked. Said he didn't appreciate being sold like a farm animal."

I flinched. "Any ideas about how to handle it?"

"I already did. I asked him when the last time was that some girl wanted him so bad she'd *pay* to be with him."

I nodded, impressed. "Good one. So do you think he's still going to take her to the banquet?"

"I can practically guarantee it."

"You're great."

He smiled. "Damn straight."

"And it's definitely your lucky day. I took deposits from Dakota Wilson and Carlton Camp." I mentally crossed my fingers, my toes—even my eyes. "You in?"

He didn't answer immediately, so I leaned across the counter. "I'll make it worth your while," I said, and added in a singsong voice, "Money, money, *money*."

He didn't jump. In fact, he did the opposite—he grabbed a rag and made big swipes on the counter. "We're talking a lot of work. And no promises we'll get lucky again."

"Successful."

"Lucky."

I poked his shoulder. "Oh, come on, Dal. Together, we can make this thing work." When he didn't smile or nod or say anything, emotions fluttered inside me, too many to count or analyze. "And I don't think I can do it alone."

Then I froze. Was there *anything* worse than looking desperate?

He was silent for an impossibly long moment. "Since you put it that way," he said, then smiled. "All right. Makes this an Ideal Opportunity for me, doesn't it?"

Okay, maybe worse than looking desperate was having your own words used against you.

"But I want a partnership," he said, dabbing at a

pesky spot on the counter. "Not you just assigning me jobs."

I nodded, embarrassed, agreeable. Relieved.

"And fifty-fifty on the money."

"Fif—" I stopped myself. I didn't like it, but I had no choice. "Okay. But remember, we might need to work some weekends. You can't be away all the time." *With her,* I added silently.

He just looked at me, like he'd heard my thoughts. "I'm not going to leave you hanging."

A sudden rush of skaters cut our conversation short, which was fine. Our arrangement was simple enough—I knew my business ethics, and fifty-fifty was fair.

Out of the corner of my eye, I spotted Lexie and figured I'd better go earn my keep. She'd already complained that I was spending too much time talking to rink workers and new clients, and I didn't want her passing that sentiment on to her mother.

But as I handed her the new laces, my mind stayed on Dal. I was relieved that he was going to be in it for the long haul, but I sure wished I'd kept the upper hand during the conversation—especially at the vague mention of his girlfriend.

I needed to be better prepared for whatever came my way, to handle the twists and turns like a pro. A good leader knew how to do the jobs as well as delegate. And I could do that. I could.

From now on, I told myself, things would be different.

I was on my cell half the night. With Dal, Dakota, Carlton—even got a beep-in from Brandon.

"Two words," he told me. "Hamstrings."

I bit my lip and listened to his tips for premium running speed, something about "static stretching" and keeping those hamstrings flexible. Critical information for me to have, though I wasn't sure why.

I was relieved when my call waiting beeped again and I was able to make a graceful exit from the hamstring discussion, only to find myself talking to some guy from my math class who wanted me to hook him up with a particular cheerleader.

Now, my palm was *always* open for cash, but this girl was sooo out of his league that it would be like *stealing* the first fifty. I grabbed a copy of my hexagon and ran through the questions, making sure he "failed."

As nicely as possible, I told him I couldn't make it happen for him and got off the phone as fast as I could. I had done him a favor, but still, I felt bad.

I was stretched out on my carpet thinking about business ethics when Suz appeared in my doorway. She was wearing her behind-closed-doors Coke-bottle glasses, but still looked pretty cute. She marched over to the mess I had made on the floor and plopped down beside me, grabbing the hexagon and a pen. Moments later, she handed the paper back with a circle in the center of the hexagon and half-circles between the numbered points around the connecting lines. The result was something that looked like a daisy.

"Tell people that every 'No' answer means a petal will be missing from their flower. And without all the petals, their love cannot bloom."

I groaned and flopped back on the carpet.

"No, no, better," she said. "You can pretend to pluck each petal with a 'He loves me, he loves me not.' "

I laughed, sitting back up. "Suz, I'm not looking for marketing just now."

My cell phone rang again.

"Maybe it's Brandon!" she said, lunging for it. She batted her eyes as she said hello. But the eagerness quickly vanished from her face, and she thrust the phone at me. "Dal," she said, clearly disappointed.

I grabbed the phone, glad it was Dal.

"Jon Keller hangs out on the quad before school," he announced.

"Perfect. See you there, bright and early tomorrow."

I hung up and called Dakota. Then I turned off my phone. As closely as I heeded the call of the almighty dollar, on one point, I was just like everyone else at school: I was a student with homework.

Twelve

The next morning, I jammed from the parking lot to the quad. While some of my energy came from the French Roast my sister had brewed, I also couldn't wait to tell Dakota the great idea that had struck me in the shower.

Only one problem. After I tracked her down and revealed my plan, she tugged her hat down and told me to "go first."

With Dal.

My eyelashes felt like they jacked up to my brows. "This isn't about Dal and me."

"Who cares?"

"He *has* a girlfriend," I reminded her.

"*So*. You're not offering to have his baby, DelVecchio. Just *do it*. I'll watch him. And if I like what I see, I'll go next."

There was no question that Dakota was going to be a high-maintenance customer, and I needed to keep the upper hand. I knew I could always explain myself to Dal later, so I nodded and crossed the crowded quad with her. A contestant had once been fired from *The Apprentice* for refusing to embarrass herself for a task, and I would not lose Dakota for such a stupid reason. Hooking her up with Jon would be the coup I needed to hit the jackpot.

Dal stood in a small group right next to Jon, talking with a couple of hockey guys. Dakota and I moved in and tried to act natural. I had to wait for the right moment, the right positioning.

It came after the first bell rang. Dal reached down to grab his backpack from the ground. I turned my back on him, then glanced back over my shoulder.

"Dal," I said, feeling like I couldn't breathe. "Stop looking at my butt."

I turned to see him rise back to his full height, those hazel eyes gazing down at me with hundreds of chocolate brown speckles.

"I *wasn't*," he said.

I inhaled, spun back around, and called back over my shoulder. "You are now."

A totally genius idea, until I had to do it. As I strode off, I was dying inside. Absolutely dying.

I thought my heart might explode in mortification as I waited for Dakota to catch up with me.

"Not bad, DelVecchio. Not bad."

"He looked?"

"I'd say he looked. You totally dared him to. How could he not?" She laughed. "And he liked what he saw, too."

He did? *"What?"*

"Yes. I know it when I see it, and whether or not he's got a girlfriend, he likes your butt."

I bit back a smile, feeling happier than I wanted to. "So you'll try it on Jon?"

She wrinkled her nose. "No, it's too out there for me. I want something more subtle, something that only plants the seed that I'm interested."

I sighed. I'd humiliated myself for *nothing*? "Let me confer with Dal and get back to you."

When I got to my locker, Yvette was waiting for me, waving and wiggling like she had to pee.

"Don't tell me," I said flatly, slipping in beside her. "You've got a mad crush and you want to hire me to help you get him."

She looked at me for a minute, then nodded. "Yeah. Are you psychic or something?"

"Just the supernatural talents that have made me what I am today," I said, not bothering to hide the sarcasm. She didn't laugh, so I went with a more even tone. "So . . . who are you into?"

"Well, considering Brandon's taken?"

Okay, my turn not to laugh. The whole Brandon 'n' Me thing was getting old.

"Lamont Barto," she said, and did one of her full-body squirms. "He's so hot."

I knew him. A senior who wore his carrot red hair all spiky. His head looked like it was on fire, but, hey—it wasn't me looking for the date. And he played hockey with Dal, and that qualified as an easy in, so why not?

"Sure," I said, and told her my fee.

Yvette didn't flinch. How was it so many people could afford my outrageous prices? "Tomorrow," she said, then strutted off.

The next thing I knew, a body was blocking mine. My locker was getting to be a dangerous place for my personal space. I looked up into Vince Hammer's eyes and fought back my irritation with him and his IM habits.

"Kate, you're coming Friday night, right?"

"Huh?"

"My eighteenth birthday. My brother's getting me a keg. You have to be there."

I wanted to tell him to shove it, that I did *not* appreciate making his invite list simply because of Brandon. But it was so much easier to nod.

"Bring a present," he said, and ambled away.

Riiiiight.

As I propelled myself back into the hall traffic, I spotted Dal's dark wavy hair. I weaved my way over to him and looked him in the eyes, trying to get an early read, but his face was expressionless, betraying nothing of what might be going on in his guy brain.

"So . . . that thing before," I said, then felt the overwhelming urge to study the toes of my boots.

"You did that for Dakota."

I looked back up, relieved. "Uh-huh."

"Yeah—it threw me for a minute. But then I was like, why would you want me to check out your butt?"

I tried to smile. Yep, good old pal Kate.

"Which is not to say it's not a fine one," he added, a similarly strained smile lifting his mouth.

"Good save, Dal," I said. "I mean, I suppose someday, somewhere, a guy might actually find me attractive." ·

I expected him to laugh, or radically change the subject, but instead, the little bits of gold glittered in his eyes and his brows pulled together in this serious V. "Whoever gets you will be damn lucky, Kate. And if it turns out to be Brandon, I suppose I can live with it."

I'm pretty sure my mouth fell open. I *know* frustration flared up in me like a match on dry, winter wood. I mean, bad enough that everyone—including my own family—considered my forehead branded PROPERTY OF BRANDON CALLISTER, but I'd told Dal how I felt about Brandon over and over. Why didn't anyone believe me?

"I'm *not* going to end up with him."

"I just think you can do a lot better."

"I know I can," I said harshly. It was like no one could hear me. I jacked up my voice for complete and final emphasis. "*I am not Brandon Callister's girlfriend.* Okay?"

I felt like my words thundered out of me, but I figured the blood pounding in my ears had probably altered my perception.

Dal broke from my gaze and did a quick sweep of the hallway. It took me a moment to realize how quiet it had gotten. How deadly quiet.

I turned around to see face after face looking my way. Staring.

Heat rose to my cheeks. Evidently I had been as loud as I'd thought.

But you know what? Good. Great. Now everyone knew what I'd been trying to tell them all along. Big whoop.

Could we all return to our own lives now, please?

"I think you got your point across," Dal finally said, and laughed.

"About time." I forced a laugh of my own. "Now," I said, and turned toward my classroom. "If you don't mind walking with me, we've got a whole lot of business to discuss in a real short time."

We fell into step together.

Because we had so many clients beginning the program at once, we decided to start them all with the same exercise. Dal had found a terrific icebreaker on the

Internet. Our client was to say, as casually as possible, "Oh, I was going to call you last night," whether about homework or some other nonincriminating thing, and try to get a read on his or her crush's reaction.

"Good one, Dal," I said as we went our separate ways. When I sat next to Yvette in class, I quietly went over it with her.

"Sure," she said. "If that's what you and Dal think will work best for us. You guys are the experts."

That made me flinch, but I gave her a strong, confident smile. Never let 'em see you sweat, said all the business journals. Even when you were swimming in it.

In the second-floor bathroom, I ran into Dakota and gave her the assignment as well. And right as I was heading back to class, I ran smack dab into some girl. I'd never seen her before in my life, but she smiled at me as if we were friends. Then, as if something had crossed her mind, a frown creased her face.

"I'm sorry about you and Brandon." She pressed her lips together.

I must have looked as confused as I felt, because she continued.

"People say you were acting real defensive out on the quad earlier, like you might break up with him before he breaks up with you."

Omigod—could this thing get any weirder? "Uh . . . thanks. But nothing happened."

"Really?"

"Really."

"I'm so glad." Her face lit up. "You two are pure dynamite together. You're totally going to be prom king and queen."

Was I in the Twilight Zone? Besides Mama's, the only time I'd ever breathed the same air with Brandon was in the stinky chem lab. How did that qualify us as "dynamite"? Things were getting stranger and stranger.

At lunch later, Dal had already heard about my and Brandon's so-called fight.

"But the good news?" he said with a smile that started on his lips and traveled to his eyes. "Somebody called him in Arizona to get the real scoop."

"No . . ."

"He assured them you two are still very much together, and he can't wait to get back to you. Although he *does* wish you'd call more."

I laughed, spitting out a huge bite of apple. Was this still Franklin Pierce High School, or had I entered some alternate universe?

I had just enough time to finish my apple and choke down a peanut butter and Fluff sandwich before Carlton lumbered up.

"It didn't go real good, guys," he said, sitting between Dal and me. "Brianne was like, 'Why would you want to call me?' I said, 'Homework,' and she said, 'Well, next time, *almost* call someone else.' "

Ouch.

"So we need a more direct approach," Dal said. "Kate, why don't you track her down and tell her you know someone who's interested in her? She might have heard about our business. See if she makes the connection to Carlton, and if she seems interested at all."

It seemed like Dal was a natural at this.

"And if she's not, Carlton," Dal went on, "we'll talk about refunding your money."

I nodded but heard myself repeat the word "talk." As much as I hated to disappoint a customer, giving money back was about as painful to me as . . . as . . . well, having a conversation with my mother.

When I walked into English class later, a couple of girls shot me sad smiles.

"Hang in there, Kate," one told me.

"Yeah, we know you two will work things out."

Aimee McDonald glanced up from her compact. She looked lost without her trail of ducklings, but I knew the minute class was over, they'd be following her again. While my life might have changed from time to time, charmed ones like hers just stayed charmed.

"Oh, haven't you heard?" Aimee said to the girls. "Brandon says they're still good as gold." She turned back to me. "I think things got blown out of proportion a little, huh, Kate?"

I nodded. She had no idea.

"Which reminds me," Aimee said, and snapped the

compact closed. "When you have some time, I need to talk to you about, you know, *that thing*."

Cha-ching.

Our teacher announced a free study period, so I moved over to the empty desk beside Aimee—best friends that we were—and got straight to work.

I was surprised she'd need help getting *any* guy—until I found out her heart was set on the basketball team's center. With his blond hair and china blue eyes, he looked a lot like Chad Michael Murray. But his utter lack of personality made him charmless and relatively friendless, and therefore nearly impossible to get next to. Quality choice.

Aimee admitted she'd made some overtures to him and had been completely blown off. And now she was ready for Plan B.

"He's probably just shy," she added.

I held back a smile. Maybe he just wasn't into Queen Bees.

I wanted another hundred dollars so badly I could taste it. But this hookup would be more like a miracle than giving Mother Nature a nudge. I wasn't sure I could pull it off. Especially not while closing the deals with Dakota, Carlton, and Yvette. What I needed was a compromise, a way to get money but keep her at bay. . . .

And that would be a Wait List.

"You know I want to help you," I said, trying to sound sincere, like we were really and truly friends.

"But I've got several clients already, and there's only so much time in the day."

Anxiety grew in her eyes, mixed with disbelief. "You're . . . turning me *down*?"

My smile was getting harder to hold back. No one said no to Aimee McDonald—ever. Except for this basketball center guy, and look at how well she'd taken *that*. But my wanting to help her had nothing to do with high school hierarchy and everything to do with my wallet.

"For you," I said, and managed a smile, "I'll make an exception. I'll put you on the top of my Wait List, next up for service as soon as one of my clients rides off into the sunset with his or her honey." I studied her face. "And the twenty you give me up front will of course be applied to the initial fifty-dollar fee."

Her frown told me she wasn't happy. But the twenty that suddenly appeared on my desk told me she'd do it my way. I slipped it into my pocket, letting my grin free.

Thirteen

After "signing" two of Aimee's ducklings and one of Yvette's friends to the Wait List as well, I had a wallet full of cash. And one cranky twelve-year-old at my side.

"You really need to talk to your mom," I told Lexie, lugging her ice skates across the parking lot. Not only did she need a tote bag, but the $3,500 for the skating competition was now way overdue. Mrs. H. had to get her head out of her book. Or whatever dark place she had it stuck.

"I've tried," Lexie whined. "You don't know what it's like. She's still totally on my case about my homework and where I go and what I eat. But it's like she doesn't care about my skating anymore."

Lexie glanced up at me, her squinty blue eyes enlarging. For once she looked her age, and unless I was mistaken, vulnerable? I felt something inside me, something suspiciously like sympathy. I knew how tough it could be to deal with a difficult mother. Especially a mother who was changing her stripes.

"How about if I talk to your mom?" I suggested. "Maybe she'll let me pick up a tote bag for you like she did the laces. What's a good time to call, when she's not normally writing?"

"Writing?" Her face settled back into her natural what's-*your*-problem frown. "She hasn't written in, like, forever. All she ever does is cook, eat, and walk on the treadmill. Oh, and yell at my dad. *When* he's home."

Why would Mrs. H. have hired me if she could have carted her kid around herself? "I'm sure she writes when you aren't around."

Lexie shook her head like I was the child. "I know a little bit more about this than you do, Kate."

I shook my head and opened the rink door, delighted to deposit her in the locker room so I could go get some *important* work done.

Mrs. Hoppenfeffer was on the treadmill when I dropped Lexie off, so I figured the big convo could wait another day.

Back home, I raced through the kitchen door, only

to have the phone thrust at me. And since anyone who was anyone called on my cell, Dad didn't even have to tell me whose voice to expect on the line.

My stomach soured as he clomped away. I was never in the mood for my mother, but now was a particularly bad time.

"Hey," I said into the receiver, keeping to my resolution not to call her Mom since she'd stopped being one.

"Hi, honey." (Clearly she hadn't picked up on the no-endearments vibe.) "How's your week going?"

"Fine." Dad and Suz weren't close, so short and sweet would do. I didn't feel the need to make nice for their sakes.

"And your little matchmaking business?"

"It's not match—" I said, then caught myself. Getting me to correct her was one of the tricks she used to engage me in discussion. I was on to her.

"Not matchmaking?" she said. "Well, what is it, then?"

I twisted the phone cord around my hand. Tight. Tighter. "A moneymaking opportunity. An Ideal Opportunity," I said, wondering if she'd recognize and react to the buzz phrase.

"That's great, honey."

I made some kind of *uh-huh* noise, which was all her vague response had earned.

"And how's it going with your bio partner?"

"Chem. Nothing to report."

"Your classes?"

"Good."

"Dal?"

"The usual."

"Well, all right." I could hear her sigh across the ocean and the continents. She was giving up. Score one for Daughter Dearest. "Just try not to work *too* hard, Kate. Enjoy your life. And remember, money's just one way of keeping score."

My back teeth ground together. *One* way! One *way*! How *dare* she—of all people—throw ambition in *my* face.

"And are you enjoying your life?" I asked her sweetly. "Half a world away from your family?"

"Oh, Kate, you know perfectly well why I'm here, and how important it is to my career," she said, sighing.

"I know you're feeding your need for more college degrees."

"That's not fair. You make it sound like it's one big party over here. All I do is study and sleep."

"But isn't that your dream life? Just you and your textbooks? No family, no responsibilities?"

"Kate," she said, restraint edging her words. "I *get* that you're angry. But remember, after I've graduated, I'll be able to command a very respectable starting salary. In fact," she said, and paused, "maybe we'll be able to upgrade your Honda to a Lexus or an Audi."

No way was I letting her bribe me. Besides, it was on

the tip of my tongue to say, *We wouldn't have needed another car at all if you were here to do your job yourself.*

With a sense of calm that surprised me, I realized we were at an impasse. Either one of us backed down now, or this would turn into a full-fledged pissing contest. I'd made my point: she was a hypocrite. And now I had other—better—things to do.

"Don't bother," I said, and let out a long sigh. "I love my car—and the fact that it allows me to take on extra jobs and make more money. So I'll totally have the five thousand ready at my graduation, and be ready to go out on my own."

Even with thousands of miles between us, I heard her groan.

"Now," I added before she could say anything else, "nice talking to you, but I need to run."

And run I did. Literally. After hanging up, I pounded up the steps, scurried down the hall, slammed my bedroom door shut, and did a face-plant on the bed. Wishing I could keep going, run until I was out of energy, anger, and memories of my mother.

Until I was the winner. No matter *how* the score was calculated.

When my cell phone rang, I suspected it was my mother, wanting to get in the last word. But the caller ID showed Chelsea. My blood pressure slowly returning to normal, Chelsea and I talked about possible outfits for her to wear at the banquet on Friday night.

After a while, Yvette beeped in to tell me that

Lamont had simply stared at her when she'd given him the "I was going to call you last night" line after school. She wasn't sure how to take his reaction. (I wasn't, either.) Then Dakota called to say she hadn't been able to talk to Jon. Should she call him? Should we wait to meet on the quad in the morning?

Then I got a call from some guy who said he'd been referred by Dakota. I offered him my Wait List and explained the fees, and while he seemed interested, he wanted to know if he could pay in installments. That sounded like trouble—and the Wait List was supposed to simplify things—so I told him to try and see if he could raise all the cash first.

With the green stuff on my brain, I yanked my shoe box out from under the bed and emptied my wallet and pockets into it. I let myself get lost in the hundreds of bills and coins. I was mesmerized—and even a little bit in love—thinking of the endless possibilities the stash represented.

Of course, after it was deposited into interest-accruing accounts and business opportunities, I wouldn't be able to play and stare and adore it. But how cool that I'd be able to see my moolah grow to greater heights (even if it was only on paper).

I'd become my own boss, with no one else to answer to, no one to take care of. I'd be free. Self-sufficient. Directed.

In a world of my own, a little voice in the back of my head shouted. Like my mother.

No, I thought, irritated, and gave my shoe box a booted kick. Not like her.

The shoe box landed with a *whomp* against the far wall, its contents flying as high as a foot into the air. I watched the bills settle, the coins drop and roll, until it all grew quiet. Until I could breathe again.

Until it was just me, my money, and my dreams.

I had my mother's blood and her drive, but that did not mean I had to end up like her: putting myself and my ambition before anything and everything else.

I'd love the people in my life. I'd be there for them—always. And most importantly, I wouldn't start a family until I could spend time with them. This get-rich-now plan was to ward off my mother's brand of selfishness, to ensure that I'd never *have* to put work or need or anything before the ones I loved.

I'd *own* the money and my ambition instead of letting it own me.

Slowly, I crawled over to the box and started refilling it with my money, counting as I went. The simple act was soothing, the very reason I had yet to do the logical thing of depositing it in a bank.

A knock sounded at the door, and my dad cracked it open and peeked inside.

His wrinkled brow told me he *got* that this scene was somehow related to my mother's phone call, so I decided to do what I had basically just done with my life savings—throw caution to the wind. For once, I would tell him what I was thinking.

"Why don't you just divorce her, Dad? You know she's not coming back."

His head didn't jerk up. He didn't go into denial or paternal mode. Instead, he bent down to help me, his hands working to form a perfectly neat stack of dollar bills.

"She *is* coming back. She went because it was the best way we knew to stay married." He handed me the stack and settled onto the carpet, crossed-legged. "She needs to be alone now. As badly as I needed *not* to be alone when we were your age."

He looked at me, the little lines shooting out around his eyes making him look so much older than thirty-six. And I decided that maybe *I* was old enough for some more unsaid truths.

"I thought—you know—you guys had one of those shotgun weddings. I mean, I've never exactly counted the months, but wasn't I born pretty soon after?"

Nodding, he ran a hand through his hair. "But Kate, no one *had* to get married back then. There were other options. Just none that I'd consider. Your mother listened, understood how strongly I felt, and married me.

"Months later, you came along, and then your sister. And Pam adored being a mother." A smile crossed his face. "She was so good at it, too. But as time passed, you girls got older, and she started to realize—and regret—the things she gave up. So I told her to go for them. College, career, whatever she needed."

"And going off to Germany?"

"I had to be supportive. If I wasn't, she might have gone anyway—resenting me—and not come back."

Words tumbled out of me, pride be damned. "But why couldn't she be happy just with us? Why weren't we *enough*?"

He shook his head. "How can anyone understand what fulfills one person and not another? All I know is that she went away to save our marriage, not to end it. And I'll be here waiting for as long as it takes."

Thoughts and feelings collected inside me. I felt sorry for Dad, and worried that he was being delusional—but I hoped for his sake he was right. For her, I wasn't sure what I felt. Besides anger, I was just plain sad for Suz and me. We'd lost our mother before we were ready, had been forced to assume her adult responsibilities. And yet, at the same time, we were just average teenagers with chores and curfews and a parent in the house. It was like we were being tugged in two directions at the same time. And as far as I could see, the only probable result of that would be a tear down the center.

I sat back on my butt, suddenly exhausted. "But what if we needed her—really needed her? I mean, had a crisis or something?"

Dad shrugged. "I'd like to think she'd come home."

I would've liked to think that, too. But I suspected Dad had more faith in her than I did.

"Well, I'm glad we had this little talk," Dad said, standing so that my eyes were level with the knees of his jeans. "Your sister's just about got dinner ready, so finish up here and meet us downstairs, okay?"

I nodded. Yep, life did go on. And sooner or later Mom would come back—or she wouldn't—and then we'd have *that* to deal with.

"Okay, Dad," I answered. "I'll be right there." And I resumed scooping money back into my box. This mess was something I could actually do something about.

Fourteen

Dakota and I met up on the quad before school the next day. The plan was for her to go with something I'd invented myself. She'd make casual mention of "your girlfriend" to Jon, and when he said he didn't have one, she'd act all yeah-right-a-hot-guy-like-you surprised.

If that didn't work, I'd "assign" them a Future Business Leaders project to do together.

As I stood with Dakota, I saw Brianne talking with a friend, animating some story with her hands. I was overdue on making progress for Carlton, so I told Dakota I'd catch up with her.

I marched up to Brianne and introduced myself. I told her someone had paid me to help him get her interest. Then I held my breath. Her eyes went all electric, and she and her friend giggled. When she asked who the admirer was, I told her it was a secret, but she'd be "hearing" from us.

It took me a good two minutes to get through the crowd and back to Dakota. Just as I walked up, she was turning away from Jon, her face glowing.

"Walk with me," she said to me, with this really odd mix of clenched teeth and a bursting smile—sort of like when rain fell from sunny skies.

"Jon," she continued, after taking a few steps, "told me that he doesn't have a girlfriend. And that in fact," she added, and clamped her hand around my wrist, "it's a bit of a problem for him. He has a family wedding next weekend, and his ex-girlfriend, who won't leave him alone, is a guest, too. He needs a date to keep her away."

It figured Jon would be arrogant enough to think the ex still wanted him. "So you said . . . ?"

"That I'd be happy to help him out and be his personal bodyguard. And he said, 'Great.' " She laughed. "So it looks like we've got our first date, DelVecchio, whether it's official or not."

I could see the dollar signs already.

"Cool," I said with a smile. Could I actually be getting good at this?

I strolled away, the satisfaction of a job well done glowing inside me. I found Dal talking with a couple of guys, sidled in close, and gave him an elbow by way of hello. The guys wandered off, and he turned to me.

"You're happy about *something*."

"Jon's taking Dakota to a family wedding!" I nudged him again with my elbow, then told him what had happened. "Are we good, or what? First Chelsea, now Dakota."

"Oh, we got lucky," he said, tearing me away from my happy place. "Dakota was in his face when he needed her. The right place at the right time."

I didn't like his attitude. "That's the point. Making sure our clients are first and foremost in their crushes' brains."

"Oh," he said, really flat. "There's a *point* to this business besides getting rich? Thanks for telling me."

Ugh. Ninety-nine percent of the time, Dal was one of the most mature guys I knew. But every now and then he could give Brandon a run for his money.

"Look, I'm as happy as you are that she's going out with him. I'll totally take the money. But don't let this go to your head."

I gazed up at his face—the face I usually wanted to see more than any other in the world. But right now? Not so much.

Still, my gaze zapped into his. And all at once, my annoyance started to melt away. Even though Dal had done a thorough job of acting smug and superior, his eyes were telling another story. They were a soft shade of hazel, bursting with green and brown specks.

For a crazy moment, I felt like I could stare at them forever.

I don't know if my expression was looking all intense or what, but a smile tugged at his mouth. "Besides, if we're making any progress at all, it's all because of me."

"*You?*"

"Sure, my smarts, my intuition. My exceptional good looks."

My mouth dropped open. "Oh, talk about letting things go to your head!"

He laughed and took a step back, like he thought I might smack him. But this wasn't fourth grade and we weren't on the playground. Still, I wasn't going to let him beat me, so I advanced, pretending that the smack was on the way. He inched back some more, still smirking, so I kept going.

Until he backed into someone. Then I crashed into him, my face squashing into his neck. I adjusted my face to get a good breath, feeling the cold leather of his jacket against my cheek, and something like a low vibration emanating from his whole body.

I knew I should pull away. Should laugh off the whole thing. But I didn't want to. Here, up close and personal with Jason Dalrymple, was the most comfortable, most natural place I'd ever been.

I not only didn't want to pull away, I wanted to dig in deeper. Had I lost my mind?

"Okay." His voice suddenly rumbled through me.

I knew that was my cue to back off. Playtime was over. But I didn't back off. And he didn't, either. We stood there, in the middle of hundreds of people. Some who knew us, many who didn't. And his arms came around my back, encircling me, pulling me closer.

Omigod.

This was the best thing that had ever happened to me. *And* the worst. I hugged back.

The first bell rang, and Dal and I dropped our arms, trying to regain some sense of normalcy.

I was on autopilot as I walked away, my thoughts reeling. How warm I'd felt inside the circle of his arms. How peaceful. How . . . well, complete.

And how wrong of me to like his touch so much, considering I was his best friend, and *not* his girl-friend. But what I would suddenly have given to have Marissa's role and mine reversed.

And the worst part? I'd been so blinded by my feelings that I hadn't looked to see whether Dal felt the same way.

Waiting for me at our locker was Yvette, near tears, her foot tapping.

"Okay," she began. "So I called Lamont. We didn't have a lot to talk about, but I thought it went okay. But just now, in the hall? I gave him this big smile and he pretended he didn't see me!"

She did this deep sniff that seemed to start all the

way down at her feet. "You had problems like this with Brandon at first, right? Until you figured out how to make him like you?"

That crack didn't exactly make me want to drop everything to help her. But . . . I *had* taken her money. And I so didn't want to think about Dal and that hug anymore.

Focus, Kate.

What little I knew about Lamont was that he was fairly laid-back—Yvette's polar opposite. "Could be you're moving a little fast for him."

"But you told me to call him."

I did? I thought I'd told her to say she'd *thought* about calling him. Crap. My clients' romantic endeavors were all starting to blend together. Maybe I needed to create a grid.

"Hmmm . . . in any case, I think we need a more subtle approach with Lamont."

"I'm paying you *all this money,*" she said, her whine turning to a whinny. "And so far, all you've done is let me make a fool of myself!"

After a quick glance around—and people *were* starting to stare—I did a maternal "Shhh . . ." thing, even putting my arm around her shoulder for emphasis. "We'll make this work, one way or another."

"*What* way?"

My mind scrambled. The Secret Admirer plan had gotten me somewhere with Brianne. Why not try it again? "I'll go talk to Lamont, tell him someone has come to me for help in getting fixed up with him."

"And he'll say, 'Tell Yvette to save her money.' I don't *think* so!"

Heads were definitely turning. And not in an oh-look-there's-hot-Brandon's-hot-girlfriend way.

"Okay," I said, putting on my damage-control hard hat. "Let me brief Dal and get the male perspective. Then find me on the quad during lunch and we'll fix this thing."

She eyed me suspiciously. "You're sure?"

"I'm sure," I lied.

"Otherwise, I get my fifty back."

My throat tightened, making it hard to respond. I nodded. Hadn't the agreement been the first fifty down, whether I pulled off the hookup or not?

I guess failing to pull it off wasn't the same thing as giving bad advice. But I told myself I wouldn't fail. I would fix this. Somehow.

She rushed off, nearly knocking down the rail-thin girl who'd once asked me about my fees. I felt a spark of hope that she had heard about my successes with Chelsea and Dakota and was going to cough up the retainer fee. But instead, she nodded hello at me and started to walk away.

Feeling generous or stupid or something, I grabbed her arm.

"Tell him," I whispered when she turned to me,

"that you almost called him last night. About homework or whatever. And then study his reaction, how he looks, what he says. That'll give you a good indication of where he stands with you."

A smile exploded on her face. "Thanks."

"Good luck," I told her, half knowing that I'd need some luck with the uncertain things in my life, as well.

The morning whizzed by in a blur, with frequent work-work conversations tangling with necessary thoughts of schoolwork. I even found Brandon's ex, Summer Smith, waiting impatiently outside my English class. Her blond hair shining in the fluorescent light, she stopped sighing long enough to tell me she wanted to talk.

"You're going to be at Vince's party tonight, right, Kate?"

I shrugged and gave her my business card, hoping she'd join my Wait List. "Just in case it's too crowded tonight and I don't see you," I said. "Call me."

Later, I met up with Dal outside at lunch.

"Where've you been hiding?"

"Hiding?" I repeated, plopping down next to him and pulling a slightly squished tuna sandwich from its plastic bag.

His gaze bore down on me, forest green. Not his friendliest color, but not a serial-killer look, either. "You didn't come out for morning break."

"I had some clients to attend to," I said truthfully.

Under normal circumstances, I would have elaborated, but the air between us held a lot more than breath clouds and tuna stink, and I wanted to clear it. "I wasn't ignoring you, if that's what you think."

"Why would I think that?" he asked, shivering inside his jacket.

"Well, you know."

He shifted his weight and his voice dropped. "Yeah." He was quiet for a little too long, looking straight over my head. "I should probably remind you I'll be gone this weekend. I'm driving out to the U later."

A stranger would have thought his response was a non sequitur, but he knew that the "you know" was my name for our too-long, too-tight hug. I realized that he thought we'd crossed the line earlier, too, and that it hadn't felt exciting or heart-thrashing or tempting to him.

Being with me had just felt plain wrong to him. The way it *should* have felt to me.

"Yeah, have fun." I took an oversized bite of my sandwich, just to make sure no more words or any miserable moans slipped out, even though I had totally lost my appetite. I was going to have to hold these new feelings for him as close to my chest as insider trading tips.

"So we're on target with all the clients, then?"

A change in the subject would have been greatly welcome at this point. I *wasn't* in complete control of our clients. Or my grades. Or my family. Or him. But it felt a lot safer to talk about Yvette and Lamont, so I swallowed and explained what had happened.

"Sounds like she freaked him out."

I cringed, unable to miss the obvious parallel. "I guess she did. So what do we do?"

He scrunched his face. "No more games or tests, that's for sure. Best thing now is brutal honesty. Have her tell him she paid you to help her hook up with him, and you gave her bad advice."

"What?"

He held up a hand. "So she tells him she's sorry, and she really doesn't want to own him or be his girlfriend or anything, she just wants the chance to hang with him a little."

"That's not the brutal truth."

"You asked for something that might work."

I studied his face. "And that would work on you?"

"If a girl I wasn't sure about was throwing herself at me?" he said, and shrugged. "And I got to choose between, say, going for coffee with her, hurting her feelings, or letting her put a collar around my neck? Coffee would be a no-brainer."

I nodded, hearing him on numerous levels. Once again, he was coming through with good, sound advice. And in a similar situation, I'd have gone for the safest and kindest option, too—most people would. Plus, I supposed it was only fair for Yvette to make me out to be the bad guy.

Still, I couldn't help internalizing Dal's comments,

wondering if he was sharper than I was giving him credit for, if he *was* tuning in to my new feelings for him.

Was he choosing the lesser evil with me, too? I mean, no way he was taking me over Marissa. Yet he didn't want to hurt me, either. So I remained forever . . . good pal Kate.

When I opened my mouth to respond, I knew full well the words were coming from my heart. "But would you ever—could you ever—start to like the girl?"

A group of people moved passed us, each of them saying some version of "Hi, Kate." I tried to smile and nod, but it was really hard, considering I couldn't tear my eyes away from Dal's face.

"If coffee went well," he answered, "if she wasn't too pushy. Yeah, it could happen."

"Even if you were already going out with someone else?"

"What?" Dal's face tightened. "Lamont has a *girlfriend?*"

"No," I said, and then laughed. Too hard. "I just meant hypothetically."

"I don't know," he said dismissively. "I can't even go there. I wouldn't encourage someone to pursue a crush on a person who was committed. That's just wrong."

I tugged on my cap, sort of wishing it would cover my whole face and body. "Yeah, of course. I totally agree."

Fifteen

When I picked Lexie up after school, I could tell she was having a hard day, too. I couldn't even get her to accept a Life Saver, and as we crossed the parking lot after practice, she didn't take her usual offense when I answered my phone, or when Chelsea stopped me for a good-luck hug before her big date.

I was getting kind of worried about the little brat, so as we pulled into her family's darkened driveway that night, I played my trump card. "I got a voice mail from Brandon a little while ago. Wanna hear it?"

She broke free of her seat belt. "Does he do lovey-dovey mushy stuff?"

I turned and gave her a look that said "In your dreams."

"Talk dirty, then?"

"Lexie!"

"Then *why* would I want to listen?"

I smiled. "Because you're the one with the crush on him?"

She sighed and inched toward the passenger door, then gave me a very grown-up frown. "Nothing lasts forever, Kate."

Yeah, I wanted to reply. *Like my patience with you.* But instead of losing my job, I got out of the car and followed her to the door. Maybe this time Mrs. H. would be available.

Lexie bolted into the house, leaving the door ajar. She must have told her mother I was waiting, because before I could knock, Mrs. H. pulled the door open and invited me in. I stepped inside the entryway, spying the circular staircase and hanging chandelier, and shivered a little as I acclimated to the room's warmth.

"I need you to drive Lexie tomorrow," Mrs. H. said as if she'd called the meeting. "Her father is unavailable." Then, as fast as she'd approached, she turned and walked away.

I stood on the Oriental rug, confused. Had I been dismissed or should I wait for her to come back? After an embarrassing amount of time passed, I fished for my cell phone, pretended to answer it, and slipped outside as if to take the call. If there was some hidden security camera, I didn't want to look like a *total* idiot. When another few minutes passed, I headed for my car, feeling as powerless with my employer as I did with my clients.

That night, I opened my chem book, knowing full well that across town, Vince Hammer's party was about to blaze into the night sky. It was one of the first times I'd been invited to an A-list event, and here I was, blowing it off.

Suzannah thought I'd lost my mind. Maybe I had. But the bright lights and demands of my newfound popularity were taking their toll on me. I was too tired to go hang with Brandon's friends and to pretend I cared about him as much as they did.

Eventually my sister went off to a friend's and Dad sank into his TV haze. I was alone, with superdull homework and a cell phone so quiet I had to check to see if it was still working. So I did what I always did when the walls closed in. I tried to lose myself in the Dow, the S & P 500, in the Trump Organization Web site—in my future.

The laptop made its usual noises as it warmed up, but for some reason, I couldn't make mine. I couldn't get any more interested in the Consumer Price Index than I had been in electron orbitals. One subject was as just-kill-me boring as another.

It was crazy. Crazier than skipping an A-list party. Crazier than telling the guy who makes your blood race to "have fun" with his girlfriend in her dorm room. Crazier than . . . well, anything I could think of.

The one thing that separated me from the rest of the world was my dream. I wasn't settling for the traditional track. I was going to make a mark, make a name, and make lots and lots of moolah. And the only way of achieving that fantastic dream was by careful planning. The amount of energy and research I put in this year would directly affect the outcome of my first big business venture, whether I doubled or tripled my college fund and set myself on track for my next Ideal Opportunity or lost everything.

There was no room for distractions. Not quasi boyfriends or best friends with girlfriends. Or deepseated fears that I might not be as naturally gifted in business dealings as I liked to believe.

No, it was not the time for any of that.

The real trouble was, I thought, staring at my laptop screen, I just couldn't figure out what it *was* time for.

The next morning, Carlton called. He'd watched Brianne and her friend jump up and down in the halls the day before over his anonymous love note.

"What's next?" he asked. "Send flowers to her house?"

I bit my lip. I'd just read an article that suggested that in matters of the heart, time spoke louder than cash. "How about you burn her a CD of your favorite songs? Then type up a playlist, and I'll give her the package on Monday. And maybe Tuesday, after she's had time to listen and really wonder, we'll reveal you."

"You're a genius!"

I laughed. "Actually, I prefer the term Love Goddess."

As soon as I hung up, the smile slid from my face. I wished I really *did* have a fail-safe plan for Carlton—six-point or otherwise. And I couldn't stop worrying that all I was really doing was setting him up for one giant fall.

On my way to the supermarket, I called Yvette and left her a voice mail. I knew Dal had talked to her before leaving for the university yesterday, and I also knew she was pretty pissed off and was demanding her money back, whether or not making me the fall guy softened Lamont's heart. I sure hoped our plan worked.

Lexie was actually ready when I drove up later, and it was clear her tongue was in fine working order again. Lucky me. From the backseat, she told me how to drive, and as we entered the rink, she proceeded to explain that what I really needed to get my business booming was to hire *her*.

"Think of me as your apprentice, Kate. I'll watch and learn, and make helpful suggestions. And when I get to high school, I'll take over the business."

I choked back a laugh. The day I needed a twelve-year-old's help was the day I admitted my parents were right and I needed college before making my foray into the business world. "Nice try."

"Okay, just let me in on a few of your secrets so I can sell them at my school."

"My secrets," I said, "are just that. Secrets. And besides," I added, lowering my voice, "they're getting mixed results."

Lexie jutted her chin. "So tell me one or two and give me a chance to make them better."

I just shook my head. She was *such* a piece of work.

As I steered Lexie through the locker room door, Chelsea was walking out. She looked pasty-faced, and her hair was all stringy again. My first thought was that the banquet had been a disaster. But that would not explain the elation that seemed to radiate from her every pore.

"Oh, Kate, the banquet was *so* great," she said, and flashed the hundred-watt smile that had probably cupid-darted Mark to begin with. "He paid attention to me, introduced me to the other guys and their dates, and told me how pretty I looked. Wow, huh?"

"Wow," I agreed.

Then she let out a sigh, and for some reason, my gaze went to the leftover mascara smudges under her eyes. "The only problem is, he isn't talking much to me today. I mean, every time I walk up to him, he seems to get real busy."

I chewed on the inside of my cheek. Technically,

she was not my client anymore. But I really *did* want everyone to be happy, and the solution to her dilemma was *such* a no-brainer.

"Well, Chelsea," I said, and swallowed. "You've definitely got the grunge thing going. And last night, you were probably gorgeous, right? You're probably confusing the poor guy."

Her brow knitted. "You're saying that the normal, regular, everyday me isn't good enough for him?"

Ouch. How to dance around *this* carefully? "No, but it seems that the better a person looks, the more the opposite sex seems to pay attention. You two *did* hook up during that breakfast when you looked so hot. And," I continued, "you've been looking great at school lately."

I could see the thoughts dancing in her eyes. Finally, she refocused on me, her voice matter-of-fact. "So the secret to your hooking-up business is being what the other person wants you to be. Not your real self."

"No! Of course not," I said. While thinking, Omigod, is it? Have I become totally superficial just to close deals?

She shook her head, then marched off. I wanted to run after her, but what if I blurted out something that made things worse?

I tried to tell myself that she just needed to calm down (and brush her hair) and everything would be fine again. But I sure wished Dal was here. He was my voice of reason, the one with the great ideas and solutions, who always knew just what to say.

Of course, he was probably saying incredible things into Marissa's ear right now. And I *so* didn't want to think about that.

Instead of heading up to my office, I took a seat on the lowest bench, with the mothers. I smiled at the group, willing them to talk to me and distract me from my life, and I kind of didn't mind getting a closer view of Lexie skating, either. The girl was *good*.

Catching myself smiling at her smooth double-axel landing, I realized I'd actually grown fond of the little whiner. And that in some ways, we weren't all that different. We both had difficult mothers, were headstrong in our pursuits, and probably had more bark than bite. Not that I'd tell *her* that—she'd likely figure out a way to use it against me.

After practice ended, I said goodbye to a few of the friendlier moms and wandered toward the locker room, only to come face to face with Mark and Chelsea—holding hands. Which was wonderful. Perfect. Relieving.

Except for the death stares they were drilling into me.

"You told Chelsea I only liked her when she had makeup on?" Mark said, and left his mouth hanging open like he had lots more to say.

"Not exactly," I said, and shifted a bunch of stuff from one hand to another. Why was it suddenly so stuffy in this rink, so hard to breathe?

"You really think," he went on, "I'm *that* shallow, Kate?"

"No—"

"If I was blowing her off this morning, it was only because I had work to do. I gotta keep my job, you know? And about me asking her out when she was looking incredible—well, it just so happened that was the day she gave me the signals that she was interested."

To my supreme relief, Lexie's coach appeared and thrust an invoice at me for her competition costs, with the word OVERDUE tattooed on top. Since I was already in groveling mode, I nodded during the brief lecture on how it wasn't his job to collect the money, and promised to deliver both the invoice and the word on to Mrs. H. personally.

When I turned back to Mark and Chelsea, they were gone. That didn't keep me from wanting the earth to swallow me whole. I grabbed Lexie, who at that moment felt like the closest thing in the world I had to a friend, and ushered her out the door.

⋅

Back home, I left a message on Aimee McDonald's cell phone that she was being moved from our Wait List to Active Status. I tried to sound all chipper and excited and in control, and not like someone who was having as many failures as she was successes.

That night, Summer called. But instead of a standard hello, she greeted me with "Why weren't you at Vince's party? And don't tell me you weren't invited. Brandon's girlfriend gets invited to *everything*."

"I was tired," I said, without adding exactly of what.

"Whatever. Look, I'm ready to sign up for your little business."

I grimaced. "*My little business* costs one hundred bucks. Twenty now, to be Wait-Listed—"

"Wait-Listed!"

"What can I say? I'm popular." After a pause long enough to drive that statement home, I continued. "But the twenty's applied to the first fifty when you move to the Active List."

She made a noise that I took for agreement. "Now," she said, "as far as the guy, I want you to surprise me. I mean—duh—we obviously have the same taste in males."

"It doesn't work that way."

"What—I pick the guy?" She laughed, but it was dry and without humor. "I can pick and *get* any guy I want. What I want is for you to use that hexagon everyone's talking about to find the right guy to make me prom queen. Someone from a different group, who'll get all his friends' votes, while I get all mine."

I made a face into the receiver. What she needed

was a campaign manager. But money was money. "You're pushing me here, Summer."

I felt her grinning over the phone line; she thought she was winning me over.

"But I'll do it," I told her. "For an extra twenty."

"What?"

"Take it or leave it."

She grumbled and hung up, but I knew I'd be hearing from her again. And that her money would look oh so good in my shoe box.

Church bells rang in the distance the next morning as I slipped my feet into my Uggs. For a moment I thought I heard another bell, too—shorter, louder—but I just shook my head and topped a pair of sweatpants with a Seattle Seahawks jersey. Perfect laze-around-the-house attire.

Suz was suddenly in the doorway, her glasses in her hand, high color in her cheeks, flicking her thumb toward the staircase.

Thoughts of Dal raced through me. Something had gone wrong with Marissa, and he needed me! Yes!

Except that the only time Dal ever talked to me about her was in passing. Like he didn't think I had enough life experience to understand the stuff they went through—or like everything between them was so frigging perfect, there was nothing to discuss.

"Dal?" I asked.

She shook her head, then took the stairs two at a time.

I rushed behind her. And a moment later, her thrill and astonishment made sense. Filling the doorway was the broad physique of my so-called boyfriend.

Brandon was back.

Sixteen

"Hey, Kate," Brandon said, and flashed a toothy grin.

I tried to make sense of his presence but came up short. I mean, (a) he was supposed to be in Arizona for another week, (b) he should have at least called first, and (c) I'd half figured that when I saw him again, he'd look different somehow, like a love interest instead of the lab partner who'd been annoying me all semester.

"Hi," I said, and tried to smile. "You're . . . back early."

"Yeah." He moved in and pressed his lips against my cheek.

From somewhere close, I heard a dreamy sigh. But it wasn't from me. Sure, Brandon smelled good and his lips were warm against my skin. But my insides—where it counted—were still coolly indifferent. So much for absence making my heart grow fonder.

He pulled back, and I noted with satisfaction that he moved entirely out of my personal space. Good little hostess that I was, I led him into the living room, where I made a fast butt-plant in my dad's easy chair. No chance of touchy-feely back-together stuff.

He settled on the couch, his shoulders rounded inside his jacket, his blue-jeaned knees wide open. It was nice that one of us seemed comfortable.

While forcing some semblance of a smile onto my face, I heard my sister scurrying off. Which was good—I didn't want her lovesick sighs turning into full-bodied moans and embarrassing us all.

"So," I said. "How'd it go?"

"Good." Another grin curved his lips. "Okay, great. A few coaches told me to go home and get working on my grades so they can try to recruit me to play for them next year."

"Terrific," I said out loud, while all I could think was what an *idiot* I had been to agree to wait for him. All I'd done was postpone the inevitable, this awful and awkward moment when I'd have to tell him this joke of a relationship was over.

My problem was, people might be paying me for hookups, but I had no *clue* how to gracefully *break* up.

"Yeah, but it was a long week," he said, and a frown settled on his face. "I'm glad to be back. I missed you."

"Uh-huh," I said, fixated on how totally clueless Brandon was. He *had* to know we had nothing in common. He *had* to have noticed I never called, IM'd, or texted him back. How could he "miss" a person he didn't know and who didn't care?

"Brandon," I said, sitting up straight.

"Babe," he said simultaneously, so that our voices collided in the air.

We both laughed and he put his hand up, signaling he was taking the reins. Didn't his mother ever teach him about ladies first?

"Kate, I came over this morning to tell you that, well, I still like you and everything, and I hate to bum you out, but I gotta end this thing between us."

I felt my eyelashes fly up to my eyebrows.

Wait. What? *He* was breaking up with *me*?

"I'm sorry. I didn't mean for it to happen. I've been crushing on you for weeks, maybe months. But last week, I got together with someone else. She was really there for me like I needed." He paused, and his unsaid words spoke volumes. "I don't know what I would have done without her."

I cleared my throat, hoping that when I spoke, my shock didn't sound like heartbreak or devastation. "You met someone in Arizona?" I said, working for an even tone.

"No, I meant on the phone. And IMs . . . and e-mails. Jenn. You know, Jenn Hammer."

My brain scrambled. Oh, sure, Vince's sister, the one who'd needed Brandon's address so she could e-mail him about some DVD.

A laugh bubbled its way up and out of me. I'd be crazy not to look at this as a blessing, not to feel relieved that I'd gotten off so easy. But wait, just for a moment, could it tick me off that he was giving me the heave-ho for a girl I'd sent his way?

"I hope we can still be friends," he said, and sounded sincere.

My feeling-sorry-for-myself moment came to an abrupt end. "Sure," I said, and settled deeper into my dad's chair, to show the same sort of casual body language he'd rolled in with.

"No problemo?"

"Three words, Brandon: just be happy."

He let out a long sigh that ended in a half whistle. "Wow. Thanks. I knew you were different from other girls." He scooted to the edge of the couch, itching to make his exit. "I don't suppose you'll help me get my grade up in chem?"

Oh, was this guy pushing it! But I saw a way to make this work for me. "Tell you what. You let me concentrate in lab, and I'll let you copy from me."

"I already copy from you."

You'd think he would've stopped while he was ahead. "Yeah, Brandon, I'll help you, okay?"

He stood, took some steps toward me, then nodded. It was *so* much better than letting him kiss me. I walked him out with an odd feeling of victory—and disbelief.

Closing the door, I turned to find my sister practically on top of me. It seemed that while she might have left the room, she had never really left the conversation. I should have been mad. But I wasn't.

"You okay?" she asked, slipping her glasses back on.

"Fine."

"But he broke up with you."

"He did me a favor."

She studied my face, sisterly concern in her squint.

"Okay," I conceded. "In a perfect world, he would have come to his senses and admitted we were never a couple to begin with. But the important thing is that this faux relationship is now officially over."

She seemed to take this in. "Does that mean if he's ever free again, you won't be mad if I make a move on him?"

I sort of laughed. "Like you ever step out of your 'safe' crowd."

She shrugged a shoulder. "It could happen."

I went to make a face, then realized she was right. It could. Running full speed at what we wanted was certainly a female DelVecchio trait. And if Brandon was ever single again and he was what she really wanted . . . well, sure, whatever.

"It's fine with me. But we'd better go run it by the hexagon, don't you think?"

She grinned and hugged me.

The phone calls started that afternoon.

Cautious at first. "Is it true?" Then more direct. "I hear Brandon's back and he's moved on to someone else." Finally, more aggressive. Like I was on suicide watch. "Do you need me to come sit with you?"

I didn't *need* anything. Except to get my focus back on the things that really mattered.

I mean, in the past week, I'd been so sidetracked I'd come close to sinking my English grade—which would have meant the death of straight As. I'd taken deposits from people I hadn't even begun to help, and had screwed some customers royally.

And let's not forget that I'd somehow developed feelings for my best friend, who was in a long-term, committed relationship. Didn't it just figure that the one guy in our overcrowded school who suddenly *did it* for me was already *doing it* with somebody else?

It was no wonder I tossed and turned for hours that night.

In the morning, I looked like the walking dead, with circles under my eyes dark enough to match my peacoat and hair I was barely able to shove under my knit hat.

As we pulled into the school parking lot, Suzannah advised me to keep my head tilted down when I walked.

The last thing we wanted people thinking was that I'd been crying my eyes out.

"This is the one time," Suz said to me, "you can truly use Mom as an example."

I eased into an open space, then turned to her. "What? Mom? Why?"

"You know how she always acts as if there's nothing wrong with her and Dad? As if her being in Germany is only about school? I mean, we all know there's way more to it."

I couldn't believe what I was hearing. "Suz," I said softly, and reached out to touch her arm. I was proud of her for being so intuitive, and yet, like watching a little kid who'd finally figured out the truth about Santa Claus, I was sorry for her lost innocence. "How long have you . . ."

She shook her head, giving me the let's-not-go-there signal. "Kate, just remember today that you're a DelVecchio. Be proud, be strong. Be—"

"Full of it?"

She laughed. "Sure, that, too."

We climbed out of the car and slammed our doors behind us. Keeping my head down as my sister suggested, I nevertheless saw a group of girls across the way, lounging by a staircase railing.

"Keep walking," Suz advised. "If they see you, they'll just rush you with questions. And who cares, right?"

"Right," I said, noticing with some surprise that

none of them—not even Aimee McDonald—glanced my way.

Inside the building, I fell in with the advancing throng. Funny, but the halls seemed more crowded than ever. If I'd been paranoid, I would have thought it was because people were stopping to gossip about Brandon dumping me. But logically I knew it was more about what people weren't doing—moving very fast.

When I finally got to my locker, I felt like I'd scored a touchdown. Yvette had the door open and was doing a whole-body shimmy out of her jacket. She'd been one of my calls last night, so I knew she had the 411 on Brandon and Jenn.

I looked at her, my muscles tensing. Any way you sliced it, the curtain was rising between us for drama. For good news (Lamont loved the confession and they were now together), for terrible news (he told her where to shove it), for Twenty Questions ("Tell me everything about Brandon and Jenn!"), or for a pity party ("You *poor* thing!").

"Hey," I said, dropping my backpack to the floor.

She glanced my way. "I hope you have my fifty bucks."

Ouch. "Lamont didn't go for you telling him I'd screwed up?"

"I'm not even trying it now."

"Why not?" A numbness was coming over me, like when you know you're about to hear something you totally want to block.

"I can't admit I went to *you* for advice."

Oh, yeah, me—Loser Extraordinaire.

But I couldn't dwell on that. The bottom line remained the same: this was business.

"All the more reason to try, Yvette. If he's at all interested, he'll try to comfort you and make you feel better for having hired a dimwit like me."

"Just bring the money tomorrow."

I hauled my backpack up on my shoulder, attempting not to think about how I'd tried to sell myself out. Or exactly how far I'd go to make this dream of mine come true.

The sight of Summer's blond hair in the oncoming rush was a welcome relief. With Brandon out of my life and Yvette about to become an ex-customer, I definitely had the time for her prom quest.

I hurried toward her, doing a little finger wave, but she looked straight through me. Was it possible she hadn't seen me enough times to recognize me?

"Summer," I called out. "It's Kate."

She halted. If the corridor hadn't been so crowded and noisy, I swear I would have heard her heels screech. I stopped, too. Someone bumped into me, swore, and carried on.

"I know who you are," Summer said to me. "Or who you *were*."

Her words connected squarely with my ego. "Well, if you still want to talk about my business—"

She cut me off with a laugh. "Yeah, *right*," she said, and sashayed off. "You are *so* yesterday."

I watched as she walked away, swallowing hard. Then I shrugged and took a step forward to try to get back into the flow of the crowd.

But no one let me in. No one acknowledged me, said hello, smiled, made eye contact, or even shot me a look of pity. Not strangers, not those with familiar faces, not friends, not clients.

It was like everything was upside down, like all the rules had changed. Like the opposite of soaring popularity was not disgrace, the opposite of love was not hate. And the opposite of being Brandon Callister's girlfriend (even his perceived girlfriend) was not simply being his ex.

It was ceasing to exist.

Seventeen

Dragging myself out to the quad later, I decided that this was how my dad must feel after long hours of wrestling sewage pipes: exhausted, bored, unimportant, and ready for comfort. Dad had his TV and his chair.

I wanted Dal.

I surveyed the huddles until I spotted him standing with a group, his hair needing a comb, his eyes dark and darting. Our gazes came together in this zip-zap thing, and my body moved toward his as if it had a mind of its own.

"Hey, stranger," he said, and opened his arms to me. "I've been looking for you."

I braced myself for the power in his touch and was not disappointed by the knee-buckling sensations that raced through me when I hugged him. But I pulled away disappointed. It had all happened so quickly and was so completely friend appropriate. Of course, he'd spent the weekend in Marissa's arms, so he was hardly needy for female affection. Especially mine.

I caught my breath and regrouped. "You heard the news, I'm sure."

"Only once or twice or five hundred times. People seemed to want to tell me about Brandon and Jenn." He shook his head. "And some are making a huge deal out of it, like as your best friend, I'm supposed to do something about it."

My hand went to my hair. I wondered if these same people could see what I'd started feeling for Dal, if maybe I hadn't been as careful as I thought.

"Kate?"

I refocused on his handsome face.

"You don't want me to confront him, do you? I mean, you've told me over and over that you don't even like the guy."

I let out a laugh, which appeared as a cloud between us in the cold. "Totally. Don't worry, Dal. If anything, I'm relieved." I was also super surprised he was offering. The last time he had defended my honor had been . . . what . . . on the elementary school playground?

"I'm glad. You're too good for him anyway." He slipped his bare hands in the front pockets of his jeans. "And honestly, I'm kind of burned out on confrontations. I feel like that's all I did all weekend."

I tried not to smile—"tried" being the operative word. "Really?"

"Marissa is dead set against our hookup business. She called it 'a crime against nature' and accused us of stealing people's money. And said we should get out before we do any real damage."

Oh, she did, did she? My eyes narrowed.

Okay, I loved the fact that I was causing trouble between them, even indirectly. And from people's reactions today, our business was on its last legs anyway. But that didn't mean I had to take her criticism lying down. Especially since she was the one getting to do the coveted lying down with Dal.

"Maybe if she was here and actually saw what we were doing, she wouldn't be so fast to judge," I told him.

"Maybe. But face it, Kate, we *have* been flying by the seats of our pants."

Sure, but no way I was giving her the upper hand. "We've been providing a service. Supply and demand. Capitalism at its finest—"

He held up a hand. Which was probably a good move, since I was working up to the kind of spin I usually felt while banging my meeting gavel.

"Mark was all pissed off last week," he reminded

me. "And last I heard, Yvette was freaking out over Lamont."

That stopped me even colder. So true. And he didn't even know that Mark was mad at me *again*. Chelsea, too. And that the Yvette/Lamont thing had actually gotten worse.

He inched toward me, not just closing the gap between us but heating the air a little, too. "How did that work out for Yvette, by the way?"

"She wants her money back." I rolled my eyes. "Okay, yeah, so there's been some mistakes. But we made two clients pretty happy. That's something." *Not to mention,* I continued silently, *that the extra time you and I spent together has made* me *happy.*

As we stood there at an impasse, Carlton appeared and handed me a CD for Brianne. Right then it dawned on me that no one else had approached Dal and me at all in the past few minutes. Not a word about the hookup biz, not even a "hi" in passing.

It was like the past week had been a dream.

I took the CD, but I had to be totally honest with him. "You *do* know my name is mud, right? And that any association with me is going to negatively affect your image?"

Carlton huffed out a laugh. "You *do* know I'm desperate, right? Senior year's ending in a few months, and I may never see her again. I'm running out of time."

"Fair enough." I offered him a hand, and he shook it. "I'll let you know when I make the drop. And you let me know if you need anything from me," I added, mentally crossing my fingers that it wouldn't be his money back.

As I walked to chem, I tried to convince myself that seeing Brandon would be no big deal. We'd left things on a good note. And he was the dump*er,* after all.

What I didn't count on was finding my so-called ex in a closed-eyes lip-lock with his new girlfriend next to our classroom door.

I drew in a ragged breath, unable to tear my eyes away. Being squashed down to invisibility wasn't enough? Brandon had to pick at the *remaining* shreds of my dignity?

Totally into the kiss, he was holding Jenn's waist like she was a delicate bouquet of flowers. As I neared, people noticed me and started stepping back. Voices dropped to a whisper. The only sounds I could hear above my own heartbeats and my racing thoughts were my footsteps across the tiles. I had a bigger audience than most of our school musicals.

So . . . how to handle this? Glare? Pretend not to see them? Make some sort of guttural noise in my throat? "Accidentally" bump into them?

All doable. But I sidestepped those ideas and went with what was beginning to become second nature to me: I tried to turn it into an Ideal Opportunity.

"Excuse me," I said, tapping cute little Jenn's cute little shoulder.

They broke the kiss. Brandon's eyes popped open and he dropped his hold on Jenn's waist.

"Hi there," I said to him when our gazes met.

He seemed to flinch, but maybe I was giving him more credit than he deserved. Jenn dropped her arms and turned toward me, too.

I let my gaze bounce between them both. "I just want to let you know that I'll be billing you. Fifty bucks for giving Jenn your e-mail address, another fifty for sealing the deal."

Around us, a few people chuckled.

"You . . . ," Brandon sputtered. "What?"

"I'm sure you've heard about my hookup business? You two are my best work of all. Not only are you on opposite ends of the popularity scale," I said, and let my gaze linger on Jenn's face, "but I was so sly at this hookup that you didn't even realize I was behind every step."

Was that a collective gasp?

"That's crazy," Jenn said.

"Think about it." Then I smiled, like I knew what I was talking about. (Yeah, right.) "And look for my bill."

I didn't wait for a reply. I cruised on into the classroom, my heart pounding, and fell into my seat.

It didn't take long for Brandon to follow and slide in beside me at our table, looking like a kindergartner who'd been benched for pushing. "Kate, I don't really owe you money, do I?"

I stared him in the eye. The big jerk. "I guess not. But you do owe me an apology. I'm fine with you being with her. But I'm not fine with you flaunting it to try to make me look even stupider in front of everybody."

Confusion flashed in his eyes. "I wasn't trying . . . I didn't think . . ."

But before he could finish his thought, I put mine together. No, of course, he didn't think. Brandon was no Einstein (a fact I'd known all along); he'd probably been making out with her simply because he wanted to.

"I'm sorry," he said, sounding sincere.

I really *did* want to make him suffer a bit longer. But finally he'd actually said two words that were worthwhile. So I nodded and shrugged.

"So what's this about a matchmaking business?" he asked, leaning back in his chair.

I smiled. "You really *have* been gone awhile, haven't you, Brandon?"

Aimee McDonald marched up to me after the last bell and demanded her Wait-List fee back. Not wanting to even go there, I pulled a couple of crumpled tens from the pocket of my jeans and dropped them in her hand. Whatever.

I made a beeline for my car. My millionaire fantasy had been crushed. Now I was a potential pauper, and I just wanted out, and for this day to be over.

Clicking my key chain remote to unlock my car, I spotted Skinny Girl leaning against the hood of another one.

"I have a date Friday night," she said, a smile pulling the sides of her mouth. "Thanks to you."

I froze. Then, gradually, as I realized what she'd said, the feeling came back to my limbs. I'd done something right? (And didn't it just figure that it was the job I'd taken pro bono?) But I contained myself. "So the icebreaker worked?"

"Oh, I didn't try it. After you told it to me, I realized the secret to your success was giving clients the tools they needed to let their crushes know how they feel. So I jumped ahead and simply told him I'd like to get to know him better. And he suggested Friday night."

I felt my eyes widen. The secret to our success? I'd had no idea Dal's and my philosophy was so, well, simple.

I let Skinny Girl's words sink in while I drove over to the Hoppenfeffers'. Lexie wasn't standing outside when I pulled up, and I realized that Mrs. H.'s SUV wasn't parked in its customary spot, either.

I threw the gear in park and hopped out of the car. The house looked closed up tight, but a legal-sized envelope protruded from under the door. My name was written on the front in bold letters.

Huh.

I grabbed the envelope and ripped it open, anticipation itching in my fingers, since it *was* payday. And
yes, inside were the twenties owed me—plus a note.

> *Kate,*
> *This is your last payment. Your services are no*
> *longer required.*
> *Amanda Hoppenfeffer*

Eighteen

No one answered the Hoppenfeffers' door.

I knew I should give up and go home. But I needed to know what I'd done. Or hadn't done.

I rushed back to my car and drove to the one other place where I might get answers: the rink.

My breathing strained from running across the lot, I entered the building to see Mark manning the skate rental counter. Dal was on the customer side, in street clothes, his jacket hanging over one arm. I hazily remembered it was payday for him, too, and guessed he'd dropped in for his check.

"Hey," I said, "have you guys seen Lexie or her parents today?"

Dal turned to me, his eyes a dark, uh-oh shade of green. "No, and I guess we won't. Mark just told me her mom called and said she's pulling Lexie from the skating program."

"*What?*" My gaze zipped to Mark's. "Why?"

"Something about the dad moving out," Mark said, and shrugged. "And the mom not wanting to bother with skating anymore."

I muttered a curse under my breath while snippets of old conversations with Lexie and her mother started to come together for me. Unfortunately, it was beginning to make sense—as much sense as anything.

"Bummer for Lexie." Dal gazed down at me. "And for you, too, since I guess you're out of a job."

The funny thing was I didn't even think about me or potential money or my future. All that got swallowed up by some good old-fashioned sympathy for Lexie.

The kid loved skating, and she had been working her little butt off to be the best. She *belonged* at that qualifying competition. More importantly, now that I knew her family life was falling apart, I knew she needed it. The planning, the excitement, the distraction.

If anyone understood this, it was me.

"How incredibly selfish *is* she?" I said to no one in particular. "Why punish Lexie because she can't get along with her husband?" I fished out my car keys. "I'm going back over there. I'm going to wait for Mrs. H. and tell her what I think."

As I turned to leave, Dal grabbed my arm. I looked him in the eye, and he was dead serious. "I'm going with you. In case you need backup."

It sounded good to me—but when had we turned into Starsky and Hutch?

Heading north on Division under a sun that slipped in and out of darkening clouds, I told Dal everything I knew about the Hoppenfeffers, and how Lexie's skating was a link with her dad.

"That sucks," he said. "To work as hard as she did and have it taken away out of spite. And to have her parents split on top of it. You and I never had to go through that, thank God, but we can only imagine, right?" He glanced toward me. "I mean, even though your mom's gone, it's not forever, right?"

I bit the inside of my mouth. Ever since my mom had left, I'd kept my suspicions about my parents' marriage tied tight inside. Was it pride? Denial? Who knew?

But in the past few days, I'd wedged open that secret place not once, but twice. And I'd *lived*, right?

Maybe it was time to open it one more time. To the one person outside my family who I wanted to know.

"Actually," I managed, keeping my eyes on the road and my hands tight on the wheel. "I don't know if my mother *is* coming back from Germany. Or whether when she does, she'll move back in with us. I don't know if anyone knows, my parents included."

The only sound in the confines of my car was the Dixie Chicks' harmony.

"Yeah," he finally said.

I glanced over at him. "You knew?"

"I wondered. You're so weird about your mom. You say you hate her, but then sometimes, you act just like her. I figured there had to be something else going on, something you weren't talking about."

I drew a breath, but my lungs felt like they were already full. "Yeah. Well, now you know."

"Now I do."

He touched the back of my hand. Just fingertips on my skin. Still, I wanted to flick him away. Did he think I was going to do something half-baked like cry—over my *mother*?

I said nothing, and eventually, he removed his hand.

Soon we pulled into the too-familiar circular drive. Mrs. H.'s SUV now sat in a ring of sunshine, looking like a gauntlet thrown down for a fight. One I readily accepted.

I turned to Dal. "Let's go tell that woman all the reasons she has to let Lexie keep skating."

He put up his hand for a high five and I slapped it, and moments later, we were marching up the driveway, gravel crunching under our feet.

When we reached the doormat, I rang, and we

waited. After some heart-pounding moments, Lexie pulled the door open. Her usual scowl and aura of extreme confidence were hidden by pink, puffy eyes.

Everything inside me tightened.

"I can't," she murmured. "I can't skate anymore. The Wicked Witch of the West—"

"Lexie!" a woman's voice boomed. Heavy footsteps sounded, then ceased. The door pulled back farther to reveal Mrs. H. in another sweatsuit, a frown dug deep into her forehead. "Go do your homework," she said to Lexie. "I'll take care of this."

Lexie gave us a desperate look, then slinked off.

Mrs. H. glared at me. "I trust you got your money and my note?"

I nodded. "But I didn't know what had happened—if I'd done something—so I went over to the rink, looking for you."

"It has nothing to do with you," she said, and took a step back, as if preparing to terminate the conversation.

"But it has everything to do with Lexie, Mrs. Hoppenfeffer," Dal spoke up. "I know you don't know me, but I work at the rink, and I've known Lexie for a while. She's a great kid and a hard worker, and she deserves to be happy." He paused. "Even if she *wasn't* a great kid, she doesn't deserve to have her passion taken away from her."

Go, Dal!

"I don't see how this is any of your business," Mrs. H. shot back. "You don't know the circumstances."

"But *I* do," I blurted out. "I know you don't like her skating. I know it's something she shares with her dad. So it doesn't take a genius to figure you're making her quit to get back at him for moving out."

Her eyes narrowed, and she exhaled loudly. I half expected steam to come out of her nose. "Not that it's *any* of your concern, but the bills have been piling up around here for months, with way more money going out than coming in. When my esteemed and estranged husband finally starts doing his share again, I'll consider the extras like ice-skating."

Fire lit her eyes. "But I promise you, Kate, after this insolence, you'll be the *last* person I'll hire to drive my daughter."

Like I'd work for a tyrant again!

I wanted to tell her *exactly* what I thought of her and mothers who put themselves first. But again, I had to pull back and remind myself that no matter how personal this felt, *this was not about me.*

"What about a grant or scholarship?" I pressed on. "What if we found a way for her to go to the New York competition for free?"

Mrs. Hoppenfeffer cackled. Just like the Wicked Witch of the West! "They don't give scholarships to people in my income bracket, honey. But if you can pull off the impossible? Sure, be my guest." Her brows arched. "Now, is this inquisition over?"

"For now," I grumbled. Then I turned away, my feet heavy, my body feeling low to the ground.

The door closed behind us with a bang, the force nearly knocking Dal and me off the front stoop of the house. He looked at me, and I looked back at him.

"What now, boss?" Dal asked.

We turned toward the driveway. Gray clouds hovered on the horizon, promising something cold, wet, and icy before nightfall. But that was the least of our problems.

"Back to the rink, I guess."

A shrill voice cut through the air. "Stop! Wait!"

I pivoted to see Lexie waving her arms over her head, making tiptoed leaps in sweat socks across the gravel. Crunching toward her, I could see tears filming the poor kid's eyes.

My rib cage seemed to tighten over my heart. I wanted so badly to help, to lift her emotional storm cloud. The one I knew so well. The one that tainted your every moment, your every movement, and even how you thought about yourself, until you were crazed to shut off your emotions, to lose yourself in something, anything, to make the pain of reality go away.

"You've got to *do* something!" she cried.

I reached out and rubbed my hands over her sleeveless upper arms to share my warmth. "We're going to your coach right now. We're going to see about getting you a scholarship for the competition."

She looked from me to Dal and back again, her eyes frantic. "No—your business. You have to use all your tricks, your hexagon and everything. To get my parents back together."

My words caught in my throat, though whether surprise or helplessness was the stronger emotion was anybody's guess. "We can't . . . do that," I said, then paused, unsure how to finish.

"Yes, you can!"

"No." I bent my knees until I was looking straight into her eyes. "I was a fake. I was just doing it for the money. Sometimes I got lucky and things worked out. But mostly they didn't, Lexie. I didn't know what I was doing."

"But if you get my parents back together," she said, using the whiny tone that for the first time did not grate on my nerves, "then everything will be good again."

I pulled her into my arms until her cheek was pressed flat against my shoulder. She felt so small and vulnerable, a world away from the thorny twelve-year-old I'd battled with for the past few months.

"I can't fix your parents' marriage. But I'll do what I can to help you, okay? And I'll be back later, all right?"

I caught Dal's eye and watched him nod.

"*We'll* be back," I amended.

Lexie's coach was doing drills, but said he could spare us three minutes. Dal and I spoke with the speed and precision of moving from the on-ramp to the fast lane of the I-90 in rush-hour traffic.

"I wish I could help," the coach told us, taking his cap off to scratch his balding head. "But Amanda Hoppenfeffer's right. They're local celebrities. People around here would laugh at the idea of their kid needing financial aid."

I shifted my weight. "What about help from the national level?"

"A year ago, maybe. Not now." He readjusted his cap. "Believe me, I am sick about Lexie missing the competition. She's a natural. I thought for sure she'd medal for our team."

I thanked him and turned away before I told him what I really thought. While he might be "sick" about her missing the competition, there was someone who was "sicker." A twelve-year-old girl who was being used as a pawn between her battling parents. Who'd just lost everything, including all hope.

If there was one thing I knew, it was that as long as I had a breath left in my body, I wouldn't sit back and let this happen without a fight.

Nineteen

Outside, sleet was falling on the Winter Wonderland parking lot.

"Where to?" Dal yelled into the wind.

"My house!"

He gave me a quizzical look.

"My dad might be able to help," I said, then looked away.

I hadn't lied to Dal since seventh grade, when I had to sit out swim class once a month and he couldn't understand why. He was older and wiser now, and like I said, sometimes he knew me better than I knew myself. He also knew that my dad had become both mother and father to me lately, so I figured this lie would fly. Which was in both our best interests. If Dal had a heads-up on what I was up to, he'd try to stop me. Worse? He might succeed.

In the car, I fiddled with the wipers to clear the windshield. "What time is it, anyway?" I asked, expecting him to read me the dashboard clock.

When he didn't respond, I glanced his way . . . to see his left arm jutted toward me, wristwatch and all.

My heart skipped a beat.

I tried to read the face on the watch, but it was like one of those dreams where you can see the numbers and letters but you can't process them into anything that makes sense. All I could think was how he'd passed the wristwatch test.

He was into me.

But then my saner side took over, pointing out how obviously amateur the test was, how it didn't take into account the kind of friends who hugged and poked at each other all the time anyway.

Yep, the test was bogus. Just like everything else about our business.

"Thanks," I managed to say, then saw his arm, wristwatch and all, move toward the dashboard, where he flipped the heater switch to defrost for me. I mumbled thanks again, and then, feeling like we needed a radical subject change to clear the air of innuendo (even though I was probably the only one who thought it was there), I offered up a smile.

"I hope you were smart enough to apply to at least one college in a warm, dry climate. These Washington winters are for the birds."

"Yeah," he said, but his voice lacked the amusement I expected. "I'm set for next year."

My stomach clenched.

Of course he was. I'd never bothered to ask where he'd applied, because I didn't really want to know. *Of course* he wanted to be with his beloved in Seattle. In the same dorm, if it was coed. In the same room, if they'd let him. Especially now that we were ending our business, just as she had dictated. They were sure to be closer than ever.

I sighed and turned up the volume on the radio. Obsessing about the lovebirds only made the pain stronger.

The house was dark. No surprise. Suz was at water polo practice, and Dad never got home before six. I turned my key in the back lock, flipped on a few lights, and steered Dal toward the fridge.

"Grab whatever you want," I said, and headed for the stairs. "I'll be right back."

Up in my room, I dropped to the carpet and crawled under my bed. Curling my fingers around the shoe box, I dragged it toward me. Then I lifted the lid and gazed at the lovely tumble of green and silver. Almost three thousand dollars in U.S. currency, but priceless to me. It was my freedom. It was my future. It was my hopes and dreams.

And soon it would cease to be mine. At the rink earlier, I'd realized what I had to do. I'd pay Lexie's bill. She had nowhere to turn and no one to help her. She needed this money a whole lot more than I did.

And somehow, moving myself back to square one felt like the only way I could put this Brandon Callister and hooking-up-business mess behind me. By forcing myself to make sweeping changes, figuring out new and better ways to make the five thou than pretending to be an expert at something I knew nothing about.

Hooking hotties—ha! I couldn't even get the guy *I* wanted. How could I have thought I'd help others?

What I'd had during this venture was guts—just not the knowledge. So I imagined if I had knowledge, too, like if I went to business school or took some college courses. There'd be no stopping me. And more book smarts might help me ward off future costly and embarrassing mistakes, too. Maybe my parents' dream that I go to college *was* actually in my best interest.

I probably needed to stop thinking of higher education as the evil intruder that stole my mother and start thinking of it as the next natural step in making my plans a reality.

Footsteps thumped up the stairs, reverberating in my chest. I looked up to see Dal filling the doorway.

His gaze swept the room, taking in the shoe box and then me. "So this is why we came here. For your money."

I didn't answer; I couldn't. I was still sane enough to

know how *in*sane it was for me to pay a rich kid's expenses with all the money I had in the world.

"Complikate," he said, his tone softening. "Think about what you're doing. That money means *everything* to you."

I searched his face, his words echoing in my ears. One of the reasons I'd initiated my Millionaire Before Twenty plan was so that down the road, I wouldn't lose sight of what was really important. But instead of preventing the problem, I had expedited and exacerbated it, making me lose sight of what was important *now*.

"Lexie needs it. And besides," I added, my voice dropping to a half whisper. "It's like the money was starting to own me. Like *I* was in the box, surrounded by cold, heartless cash."

His gaze swept over me, his eyes a placid, dollar-bill green color, which told me he respected my decision, wasn't choosing to fight. "You're sure? You know, you can't change your mind tomorrow and get it back."

"I'm sure," I said, hoping I was. I stood on slightly shaky legs, replaced the lid, and tucked the box in the curve of my arm. "Let's take this to the coach, then go give Lexie the good news."

I expected him to turn and head out. Instead, he pressed his palms on the sides of the doorjamb and leaned forward, like he was holding up the doorframe.

My heartbeats accelerated.

"I owe you an apology," he announced.

An apology? If his posture wasn't enough to stop me in my tracks, his words were. "For what?"

"When I said you were like your mother. She would never put someone else's interests first. Especially not some kid who mostly got on her nerves."

Feelings I didn't even know I had started arriving and demanding attention. I realized I could cry. Or get mad. Or *something*.

"You're an incredible person, Kate, a way better person than your mother will ever be or deserves in a daughter."

Emotion filled my throat. Wow. But while I was supertouched that he thought so much of me, I did not want to think about my mother right now. I didn't want to think about anybody. Except us. Dal and me.

His hands left their security posts and reached out to me.

I stared at him for the longest moment of my life. Then I slipped the shoe box onto the nearby desk and fell into his magnetic pull. Locking my arms around his back, I pressed my head into the hollow of his shoulder.

Adoring him.

Oh, God. Being with him like this . . . it was so wrong. It was so right.

His lips brushed my forehead in a friendly kiss, sending tingles through me—and the ominous feeling that something like lightning was going to strike. Something crazy, something freaky. Something that would do irrevocable damage.

I had no choice but to step away. He was *hers*. And the last thing I wanted was to do something we'd regret, something that would drive a stake into our friendship.

I realized that without Dal, my life would lose its meaning.

"So," I said, attempting to swallow but finding I needed saliva for that. "Should we get going?"

He paused, then reached for the shoe box. "Your money, your call. How much do you have in here, anyway?"

"Almost as much as we need. Plenty to hold her spot. It'll give us time to figure out how to get the rest."

He walked down the stairs ahead of me. "Let's make a pit stop at my house," he called back. "I've got some money, too."

"No way," I told him when I caught up with him on the landing. "You need your money for college."

"Not really. I'll be living at home and hopefully still working at the rink."

"What are you talking about? You can't commute to the U." Seattle was on the other side of the state.

"I didn't apply there. I knew it wouldn't work out."

"Financially?"

"Well, that, too," he said, and did a throat-clearing thing. "What I really meant was between Marissa and me."

My eyes shot open. I must have looked horribly in-quisitive or at least in some kind of pain, because Dal seemed to feel the need to explain.

"Look, it was fun with her at first. The homecoming dance, and then some dates. She was a senior who liked me, and how cool was that? And later, it was exciting to have a girlfriend away at college, to go visit with no parents. But take the fun away, and it was just Marissa and me. Two people who liked the idea of being together better than actually being together."

I tried to act as normal as I could. "You sound like you broke up."

Shifting his weight on the hallway linoleum, he nodded. "Yeah, we did."

Omigod. If I was dreaming, I didn't ever want to wake up. If I was awake, I didn't ever want to sleep again. Finally, finally, Dal was free!

Still, I knew I had to keep my cool. "I'm so sorry," I managed to say, lying to him for the second time that afternoon.

He paused, his gaze all over my face. "You don't seem all that sorry."

"I—don't?" *Frown, Kate, frown!* "I guess I'm surprised. And," I said, thinking fast, "worried that it had something to do with our business?"

The lines eased in his brow. "Well, yeah. Partly. She's always been a little jealous. I did a stupid thing early on, admitting I'd asked you to homecoming before her. She never got over the idea that she was second best to you. So yeah, then with her suspicions about you with our business . . . everything just blew up."

I frowned again, hoping I looked sincere. Then, since oh yeah, we needed to get to the rink, I started backing toward the kitchen and the back door.

"Just promise me something, Kate," he said, following, poking my shoulder from behind. "If I end up without a prom date, and you don't have one either, you won't call me a coward for asking you."

That stopped me dead in my tracks. "No! Well, I mean, not again. I mean," I said, and I laughed. Then I realized that the fuss, the hair, the nails, the dress—the money—it would all totally be worth it if I got to be in Dal's arms. "Yeah, I'd love to go with you. If neither of us has dates."

"The funny thing was," he said, shifting the shoe box from one arm to the other, "I really *did* want you to be my date for homecoming. I was asking for real. I only asked Marissa to save face."

Memories of that conversation slam-banged into a recent conversation, when Skinny Girl informed me that the underlying secret to my business's success was getting the crushes to know how the clients felt.

I hadn't known Dal *liked me* liked me when he'd asked. But would it have made a difference?

Ummm . . . I wasn't ready for him, so probably not. Not then.

But I thought about Mark with Chelsea. Jon with Dakota. Skinny Girl and her guy. Even Dal and Marissa. They'd gotten the message that the other was interested and taken a chance.

Did I dare take my own advice and tell him how I felt?

"I'm sorry I gave you such a hard time," I managed to say. "It won't happen again. And I'm really glad you're sticking around next year. I'm not ready to become e-mail friends yet."

"You're the one doing the leaving."

"Not necessarily. For all you know, I'll end up at the community college, too, learning how to mount an aggressive campaign on the finance world."

"I love it when you talk business, Kate."

"Yeah, well," I said, and laughed. "I love a lot of things about you, too. And I have for a long time."

My heart stopped. I expected him to laugh and launch a fastball right back at me. That was what Dal and I *did*, right? We were best friends who joked around about almost everything, even the things that cut a little too close to the bone.

But he didn't laugh. He didn't talk. He didn't poke me. He didn't do anything but stare into my eyes. "For *how* long?" he finally asked. "A week? A month?"

I knew if I was ever going to do it, it was now. "I don't know, exactly. You've sort of grown on me."

His mouth tugged upward, like he was trying to smile, but something was keeping it from completely coming through.

Then I figured, Oh what the hell? "And those days out at the lake last summer, well, I'd have to be blind not to have noticed you."

He smiled and did a he-man fist squeeze. I was sure that inside his jacket, those million-dollar abs went rock hard. (Gulp.) "Yeah, I was showing off for you a bit."

"You were? But Marissa . . ."

His face seemed to freeze-frame, and it was almost like his eyes shifted to a softer hue. "Kate, all you had to do was snap your fingers," he said, his voice low and husky. "And I would have been yours. Don't you know how I've felt about you since . . . forever?"

Thoughts and emotions clouded my head—but nothing would keep me from responding at that very moment.

I grabbed hold of his hand, and laced my fingers with his, for the first time touching him without guilt, without caution. And with all my heart.

He sidled up next to me. Close. "Hey, you know how I went searching for tricks and tests for clients?"

I nodded, vaguely following along.

"Well, I found another one, something called the Ten-Dollar Kiss, and I've been saving it to try out on you."

My insides fluttered, and I'm sure I smiled.

"You bet the girl ten bucks that you can kiss her on the mouth without your lips ever touching hers." He turned and inched toward me. "Okay. Now remember, I win, you pay me. I lose, I pay you."

I nodded, anticipation causing a fireworks thing in my veins.

His mouth, his lips, his breath, his total, hunky Jason Dalrymple—ness grew closer. And closer. Till I thought the sheer anticipation might be the death of me.

Was this the trick? You drive the girl so crazy that *she* kisses *you*?

But before I could make my move, his mouth came over mine in a nerve-numbing, mind-bending, take-me-to-the-moon kiss. One that broke our hand-hold and sent my arms flying around his neck.

Once I could breathe again, I nuzzled him with a lazy smile. "You owe me ten dollars."

He grinned. I normally didn't *do* gullible, but I normally didn't kiss the love of my life, either.

"Let me run a tab," he said, and kissed me again.

Moments later, gazing up at my amazing friend, I knew I had something money could never buy. And that when I thought about the past couple weeks, I had to admit I wasn't a *complete* failure at my business. After all, I'd made a little bit of money that I didn't have to give back.

And I'd hooked myself the hottest hottie of them all. At least to me.

Twenty

Five Months Later

The commencement committee was smart enough to plan the ceremony after the sun had set behind the football stadium, but eight hundred graduates and three or four times as many guests in any confined area generate a stifling amount of body heat. Factor in black caps and gowns, and our class was as antsy as any to toss our tassels and head for the hills.

Dal caught up to me as I was attempting to make my break. "So when are you going to show me what's under your gown?"

Anybody listening would have thought the

worst . . . or maybe the best, depending on the point of view and the fact that we'd been a totally solid, committed couple since right before midterms. But I knew exactly what he was talking about, and there was no time like the present to show him "the real me."

I backed into an empty row of folding chairs and shrugged the gown off to reveal a pink spaghetti-strapped dress.

He frowned. Not because of what it was; because of what it wasn't. Not a business suit.

"You didn't make the full five thou?" He sighed. "I'm sorry, Kate. Especially after the million hours behind the snack bar lately. Not to mention the interest you got from Mr. Hoppenfeffer when he paid you back for Lexie's competition fees."

I shrugged.

"Look, I know I told you not to come to me if you were short. But I want to help. How much do you need?"

"A little over a hundred. And thanks for the offer, but I don't want it. I pulled off the As, and I'm this close," I said, holding two fingers together, "to what my parents wanted. So if I can't talk them into cutting me slack on what amounts to a measly two percent, then I don't have the stuff to start making my first million yet."

He studied my face, probably for hints of disappointment. What I hoped he saw was the same determination I'd been showing all year. Just tempered by a bit of experience and reality.

"Oh, well," he said. "There's always the C.C."

I reached for his hand. "I've already enrolled. Even if I *get* the money, I've decided that 'student by day, entrepreneur by night' has a certain ring to it."

He smiled. "Sounds sorta sexy."

I laughed and picked up my graduation robe, and together, we headed toward the bleacher exit. I'd agreed to meet Dad and Suz at the car.

With the place so packed, I almost missed the dark-haired lady standing off to one side, holding the balloon bouquet.

Almost.

Then her gaze seared into mine—two sets of brown eyes, the exact same shade, just a generation apart.

Emotion filled my throat. "Mom . . . ," I said, abandoning my resolution never to call her by that name again.

She really *did* come home. The bull about her plane getting delayed on the East Coast—it wasn't bull. She hadn't been calling from Frankfurt after all.

"There's my favorite graduate," she said, and gave me a hug so hard it hurt.

I strong-hugged back, returning the favor. Then, completely at a loss for words, I said, "Do you remember Dal?"

"Of course, Kate. And if I didn't, the fact that you've gushed about him in every conversation for months now would have jogged my memory."

I wanted to bury my face in my hands. Did she *always* have to embarrass me?

But then I realized: yeah, she did. This was my mother. Over-the-top in so many ways. But not heartless, and not cruel. Just . . . self-absorbed and disconnected.

She did what she felt she needed to do to keep growing, to keep moving forward.

Just like I did.

That still didn't mean I liked her methods. But maybe if we spent enough time together . . . well, hey, she'd shown up here, so anything was possible.

"Nice to see you again, Mrs. DelVecchio."

"Goodness, you're a high school graduate now, Dal. An adult. Call me Pam."

I eyed her, wondering if she planned to treat me with equal respect. Only time would tell.

The three of us moved with the pack into the parking lot, where Mark and Chelsea fell in with us. They were Dal's and my one success story, the only client couple who'd made it through the school year, who seemed to want to be together enough to work at it. And yes, Mark still glared at me sometimes, and Chelsea spent too many days looking like she'd just woken up, but who said Dal and I were perfect, either?

Well—okay—the hexagon did. When we answered the questions, we got solid lines that connected at every point. I supposed the diagram *could* be considered biased, since I was the one who constructed it, but who cared? Maybe Dal and I were works in progress on our own, but we were a perfect match.

I slipped my hand in the crook of his arm and watched him smile back at me.

Any way you looked at it, being with a guy who loved you, flaws and all, rated up there as an Ideal Opportunity not to be missed.

Jari Blakely Kirkwood

Tina Ferraro was too consumed by her high school social life to create a time line for making her first million. In fact, one enduring marriage, two books, and three kids later, she's still waiting for popularity and the big bucks to arrive. In the meantime, she lives in front of a computer in Los Angeles, writing new stories and chatting with her readers. Check out her first novel, *Top Ten Uses for an Unworn Prom Dress,* and her Web site at www.tinaferraro.com.